LOOK DOWN ON THE STARS

By
Stan Potts

Author of "The Potts' Factor Versus Murphy's Law"

LOOK DOWN ON THE STARS

By
Stanley Potts

Author of "The Potts' Factor Versus Murphy's Law"

ISBN 1-931291-30-6 (softcover)
ISBN 1-931291-31-4 (hardcover)

Library of Congress Control Number 2003105397

Published in the United States of America

First Edition

ALL RIGHTS RESERVED
No part of this publication may be reproduced, stored in a retrieval system, or transmitted in any form or by any means without the prior written permission of the copyright owner or the publisher.

STONEYDALE PRESS PUBLISHING COMPANY
523 Main Street • P.O. Box 188
Stevensville, Montana 59870
Phone: 406-777-2729

Stani (my daughter) and Chris Malmgren (my son-in-law).

ACKNOWLEDGMENTS

•To my son-in-law, Chris Malmgren, for the cartoon drawings for the chapters with no pictures. Chris was a top collegiate football player with the following impressive credentials:
 1. First team Kodak All American.
 2. Second team, AP Division II All American.
 3. Big Sky Conference 1977 Defensive Player of the Year.
 4. All Big Sky Conference, 1976-77.
 5. Boise State University, Most Valuable Player in 1977.
Chris is the art teacher in the Hailey, Idaho, public school system.

•To Tom Archer for the caricature of yours truly in the chapter on Bar Stories.

•To my granddaughter, Jenny Black, of LaGrande, Oregon, for typing and putting great quantities of the book on computer disk from my handwritten scribbles. Tough job! I also have trouble reading my handwriting.

•To Mary Branscomb of Lamoille, Nevada, for permission to use her story on Paiute Indian Chief Frank Temoke and to Farm Times Publications in which it was originally published. Frank and I team roped together in north-east Nevada rodeos. He brought his grandchildren to the high school rodeos while my daughters were competing – a great friend and an important link to the past

•To Don Farmer of Elko, Nevada, for use of his painting of Frank Temoke. Joy and I are privileged to own copy #112 of 275. Don was a top saddle bronc rider in the Professional Cowboys Association in the 1960-70 era and is now a fine western artist. Frank was a strong mentor to Don while Don was growing up and I also judged several rodeos where Don was competing. An old friend of mine.

•To Joe Ausich of Mackay, Idaho, for the use of his photo of Tommy Ding, old-time mining hermit picture and the picture of my grandparents, Ada and Herb Gray at Cliff, Idaho.

•To Brian Edgerton for Siwash Gulch pictures after his successful, double tough sheep hunt in 2001.

•To Wilde Brough of Wells, Nevada, for his picture of the weird shed elk horn in the Photo Section. Wilde guided and cooked for me many years ago and is now a rancher and outfitter in Clover Valley, Nevada, where we used to live.

•To Christine Hendren for the Stoddard Bridge crossing and the picture of Gus and Shorty.

Table of Contents

Acknowledgments 3
Foreword 7
Introduction 9
Dedication 11
Chapter 1
Look Down On The Stars 25
Chapter 2
Little Boy and Indians 27
Chapter 3
Little Boy and Fire 31
Chapter 4
Trading Posts in Arizona 33
Chapter 5
Billy Finley and the Roped Cow Fiasco 37
Chapter 6
The Lightning Strikes 41
Chapter 7
Tommy Ding 45
Chapter 8
Mistaken Identities and Mining at Cobalt 49
Chapter 9
Highway Patrolman Stories 57
Chapter 10
Rodeoing Stories 67
Chapter 11
Get Rich Quick Schemes 73
Chapter 12
The Frank Temoke Story 77
Chapter 13
Poker Games 81
 •The Weiner Pigs 83

Chapter 14
Wild and Mild-Wild Hunts and Mountain Trips 85
- Sadie The Mule 85
- The New Jersey Hunters 86
- Come In Albuquerque 89
- Jingles 92
- Ken Johnson and The Rocket Mule 94
- Constipation Ridge 96
- How Do They Know? 100

Photo Section 103

Chapter 15
More Hunts – Most "How Not To Do It!" 117
- Snow Blind 117
- Big Bull, Big Bucks and No Meat to Pack! 120
- Big Bull 122
- Big Buck Number 1 123
- Big Buck Number 2 124
- White Creature In The Dark 125
- The Albino Lambs 127
- Pittsburgh Pirates Sheep Hunt 128

Chapter 16
Bar Stories – San Francisco and Chicago 135

Chapter 17
Mule Days 139

Chapter 18
Mustanging 143
- The Shorty Prunty Horse Catch 143
- How Not to be a Mustanger 146
- Roping The Mustang Colt 149
- Spruce Mountain Bill 150

Chapter 19
1924 Outfitted Trip in The Frank Church Wilderness 155
- The Diary of Pete Snedecor 155

Foreword

When I first heard, some months ago, that Stan Potts was working on another collection of stories emanating from his lifetime of outfitting and hunting and ranching and rodeoing and poking around over the last sixty or so years in the wildest parts of the American West, my only thought was "Wow, can the world stand any more of these tales from a man whose life has been lived – barely, sometimes – about as close to the edge of total fulfilment and ultimate disaster, simultaneously, as one can imagine. After all, I know from personal experience that the so-called "Potts' Factor" isn't so-called at all. It's a real phenomenon, an ever-present aura that overwhelms you with the sense that when this guy, Stan Potts, is around, things aren't just likely to happen – *they're going to happen!*

Stan, of course, is world-renowned as one of the great elk and bighorn sheep hunter-outfitters of the last half-century out of the wildest parts of the Idaho Primitive Area – now called the Frank Church Wilderness. He's also renowned as the author of a marvelous book about what he calls some of his adventures and misadventures over a lifetime in that country, which he titled *"The Potts' Factor Versus Murphy's Law."* When published a couple of years ago, it met with warm public acceptance by those who knew of him and his wild-country escapades and rambled through its first edition into a second printing fairly quickly. It was not only an incredibly unique, individualist look at a life of total freedom that Stan and his wife, Joy, lived in their beloved wild country of Idaho, but also of those who he took into that wild country and who came to share with him the same love for it that he holds.

All of them, I'm sure, and all of us who have come to know him – I worked with him helping put his first book into publishable form – soon realize that when you deal with the enthusiasm, the unbounded joy for the outdoor life, the unquenchable quest for adventure and life time-and-again pushed to the edge, that Stan Potts is indeed someone very special.

He has to be, or he wouldn't have survived. Numerous plane crashes, falls from precipitous mountain ridges, remote-area hunts pushed beyond the edge of hunger and physical deprivation, and, always, a spirit to reach beyond that next ridge – to explore and do something most men fear to try.

As we learned in *"The Potts' Factor Versus Murphy's Law,"* this life-long, hell-bent quest to live life to the fullest almost cost him his life – not several, but many times. And yet, across that entire time, Stan and Joy Potts, and their children, maintained a coherent, unified, close family; that's part of his unique story: his family has shared with him this fascinating life lived close to the earth, always working as a family to make a living out of the good, wild country they so deeply love.

The remarkable thing we learn from the stories that Stan shares with us, not only in *"The Potts' Factor Versus Murphy's Law"* but also in this new book, *"Look Down On The Stars,"* is that as strong as the Potts' Factor is, Stan Potts the person, the man, is stronger. He is, truly, a life force in his own right and we're indebted to him for letting us share these insights into the events, the relationships, the observations and conclusions he's made over the years.

"Look Down On The Stars" cuts across the gamut from the incredibly unusual to the wildly humorous, from the open-eyed wonder of a young boy coming to grips with changing times to a grown man insistent on sharing the story of a good friend and rodeoing buddy, a Native American, who, like Stan, was himself bigger than life. It also lets us go along with Stan on some of the most harrowing big game hunting adventures one might imagine, and then sets us down alongside a rambling mountain stream to contemplate what it means to the human spirit to be in some of the wildest country to be found on the North American continent. That's the power of these stories that Stan shares with us – we're there, with him, on the edge of what it means to experience the awesome, fulfilling beauty of the wilderness. He, indeed, takes us from the first chapter onward to that place when, with him, we climb to the highest of remote mountain peaks and then spend the rest of our time, with this book in our hands, literally looking down on the stars...... It was a trip I really enjoyed, and I trust that you will, too!

Dale A. Burk
Stevensville, Montana
May 18, 2003

Introduction

When I wrote my first book, ***"The Potts' Factor Versus Murphy's Law,"*** *I assumed that it would probably be my only literary attempt. However, it is now in its second printing and has been mildly successful. Also, so many of the people who know me and have a copy have read it and called or written and said, "How come you didn't tell about . . . . (whatever wild story they remembered or were involved in since these experiences began unfolding)?"*

Accordingly, this is my second attempt to capture some more of these experiences. Once again, I apologize to those of you that might possibly surface in some of these adventures!

By the way, I have had another life flight, totaled my "Kit Thing" airplane by catapulting in it into the Salmon River, and sold my outfitting business – so there may be a sequel to this book!

Hope you enjoy it.

Stan Potts
Shoup, Idaho
May 1, 2003

This pretty little lady
Was born in 1903.
She's many years our Mother
And a friend to you and me.
Now all within her family
Would invite you one and all,
To help celebrate Birthday 90
At the Mackay Legion Hall.
Now the party's on—come
　rain or shine.
And with coffee, cake and
　punch.
Her old friends she'll want to
　see again
(And we hope there's be a
　bunch!)
So mark it on your calendar
On July 17th from noon to 4.
Then come and reminisce and
　visit with
Old friends from near and far.
　　　~ ~ ~

Marlene Huebert –
Charles Potts
Don Gray – Stan Potts

DEDICATION

I am dedicating this book to my mother, Sarah Gray Potts.

After you read it you will have a whole new meaning of the word, "Dedication!"

Some of the dates and places in the following tribute to my mother are written by different people and do not necessarily jibe exactly but are for history and your enjoyment.

The first known picture of Sarah Gray Potts, taken in 1904. She is held by her uncle, William Alfred Gray, in the far left of the picture. Her father (Herb Gray, my grandfather) is on the tractor at the first threshing in the Lost River Valley.

She was born July 14, 1903, just six months before the Wright Brothers first airplane flight at the family ranch near Darlington, Idaho.

She was a lifelong educator in the public school systems of Idaho and Nevada. She received a teaching certificate from Idaho Technical Institute (now Idaho State University) when she was nineteen years old. This allowed her to start and continue her teaching career while pursuing her formal education for the next FIFTY-TWO, yes 52 years!

Nearly all her teaching jobs were in small, rural, one-room schools and teaching all eight grades.

Sarah Gray Potts in 1919 with a stylish horse hair hat.

Her first teaching job at nineteen years of age was at Forney, Idaho. She lived with the O'Connor family and taught their kids.

Through the years she continued her education with correspondence courses, summer school and attending Idaho State University.

She graduated with the class of 1975, SEVENTY-TWO years after she was born! Newspapers across the country had front page pictures of mom getting her diploma along with a big kiss from the President of Idaho State University!

The ironic part of this story is that she was forced to retire from teaching, because of her age, the year she graduated!

Besides Forney, Idaho, other Idaho schools where she taught were

Iron Creek, near Salmon, Patterson in the Pahsimeroi Valley, Alder Creek in the Big Lost River Valley and Clyde and Cedarville in the Little Lost River Valley. She was also a substitute teacher for the Mackay schools system.

In Nevada she taught at McDermott, O'Neil Basin, Jiggs and Jackpot.

She was teaching at Jackpot when she was forced to retire because of her age. Incidentally, she fought it to the bitter end. She loved to teach!

After retiring from teaching, she went to Los Angeles, California, and got her real estate license at age 73.!

While I and my brothers and sister were growing up on the ranches at Mackay, Idaho mom had a lot of ventures to help stretch the few dollars that rolled our way.

Mom always raised lots of chickens. They would come in each early spring on the railroad in big partitioned, cardboard boxes. Now these little guys were fresh out of the egg and didn't know much about anything.

Each one had to be taught to drink. You held it and dipped its beak

A picture of Sarah Gray Potts taken in 1980, with Mt. McCaleb in the background.

in a pan of water and then let it swallow till it got the hang of it. Diced-up hard-boiled eggs was there first food and they sometimes had to be taught how to eat it.

We also had milk cows and sold milk and cream to the creamery in Arco. A lot of the cream came out of the separator and mom made butter, cottage cheese, regular cheese and whipping cream.

She had a delivery route in town and a couple times a week would deliver some of and or a combination of butter, cheese, cottage cheese, whipping cream, frying chickens all cut up, stewing hens and fresh eggs.

This was where our family's "butter and egg money" came from!

Oh, she somehow was able to apportion a few quarters from the meager income train for an occasional show ticket and treats for us kids.

You were a great lady mom and we all miss you .

The following tribute to mom was written by my daughter Robyn Maxfield after mom's death on November 20, 1995.

ROBYN'S TRIBUTE

I'm not a speaker, I'm a writer, I'm a writer because I'm a reader, and I'm a reader due in large part to Grandma Potts.

Thinking back, she influenced me in ways I didn't even realize until now. When she taught school at O'Neil in Nevada, she introduced me to what is now my favorite childhood book, WHERE THE RED FERN GROWS.

Not long ago Grandma told me about a young, male teacher from Jackpot who had asked her to recommend a book to read aloud to his students. Grandma recommended WHERE THE RED FERN GROWS. "But", she cautioned him, "be sure to read it to yourself first, It's pretty sad."

"No", he said, "Sad stories don't affect me."

Well, if any of you are familiar with this book you know it's about a young boy and his two coon-hounds – and any story about kids and dogs is bound to be sad.

Grandma said this young man, his eyes red and puffy, was pretty humble when he returned the book.

You know, there are all kinds of grandmas in the word. Grandma Potts wasn't what I'd call a cozy grandma – my cozy grandma is right there, Marion Blume – you know the kind that conjures up memories of warm fires in the fireplace, Christmas dinners and church outings.

Grandma Potts is what I call my "Traveling Grandma." She always had a metal bar affixed above the back seat of her car absolutely stuffed with her hanging wardrobe, and she never stayed in one house for long.

I was very young when Grandma and Verl divorced; I don't remember them being married at all – so Grandma was my first introduction to an independent career woman, at a time in the '60s when I'm sure it was frowned upon. But in the '70s, as a teenager, I remember how proud I felt watching her accept her college diploma at the age of 72.

This past year was hard on Grandma, losing her independence, her leg and her oldest son. That's why I remember most the grandma of my youth – the tall, energetic redhead who loved to dance.

Don't you think there is a tall, energetic redhead dancing right now in Heaven?

This story of my Mother's early years was written by her a few years prior to her death.

My School Days

School was a problem when I was growing up. There were two schools about the same distance from where I lived, which was about three miles. There was only one way for me to get there and that was for my father to take me on horseback and then pick me up when school was out. We had severe winters then and the time to be going to school was about eight and then out at four. In the winter that was the coldest part of the day. We usually had eight months of school.

My grandparents lived in Mackay at that time so it was decided that I stay with them and go to school. That way I could walk as it was only a block. Everything went very well for about two weeks. By that time I was so homesick for my folks I wouldn't eat and from what they told me I cried a lot. My folks come up to see how I was getting along and also by that time I had the croup so they, being as lonesome for me, I guess, they took me home AND THAT ENDED MY first year of school..

I had a set of blocks with the numbers and both large and small letters on them so with the help of my mom and dad I did progress a little. By the time school started the next year my dad had decided to take me to one of the schools. It was an old log building that my mother and her brothers and sisters had gone to school in. It was heated by a wood stove

This photo of Sarah G. Potts receiving her education degree at the age of 72 from Idaho State University President William E. Davis appeared in the Idaho State Journal.

and about all the older boys got done was chop wood and carry it in and keep the fire going and as I remember we were never very warm unless we were lucky enough to have a seat close to the stove. The seats were about three times as large as the ones they have now and at least three pupils sat together, and I am sure there was a lot of foolishness going on. I got to go until Christmas and then it was to cold for me to ride. I had managed to get enough out of that time that by the time the next term started I was put in the second grade, but the same thing happened again. Just four months and I was kept home for the rest of the year.

At the beginning of the next year my folks decided to board the teacher. By that time she stayed with us and drove one horse on a single buggy and took me to school. I was far enough advanced that she put me in with her third graders and by, helping me some at home I did fairly well. By February her sister became ill and she was called to Spokane, Washington, and didn't come back. By the time a substitute teacher was found I had the whooping cough and that was the end of the third year.

The other school I mentioned was near a post-office and small grocery store. My folks decided to take me there as it would be convenient for picking up mail and essential groceries. I couldn't go by myself although I did ride alone because I would have to cross Lost River and in those days it usually froze over at least nearly across so it was sometimes very dangerous. I was put in the fourth grade and as I could read pretty good for the schooling I had. I read with the fifth graders and spelled with the sixth. Well, I finally made it through a complete school year and by the time school had started the next year a bridge had been built across the river and I could go by myself.

I went back to that same school and was put in the seventh grade. I could do everything but math. I had missed out on the basics some place along the line but fortunately the teacher we had this year was very strong in math. Of course, I practically had to start back about the fourth grade to get the fundamentals but she didn't let me slide by until I understood what I was doing.

I made it through another complete school year and felt that I was ready for the eighth grade. A new young teacher just fresh out of Normal School and a city was hired for the old log school. Everyone thought she would be so much better that the older teachers they had had there before as most of them lived right in the community and had but very little teacher training.

Well, that was a sad mistake. She had no idea what a rural school would be like with about twenty pupils ranging in ages from six to sixteen. The older pupils just made a mockery of her by asking silly questions that had no meaning just to embarrass her. She had absolutely no discipline whatever and by mid-term my folks had sold their ranch and were moving to Blackfoot, Idaho where the school would be only a quarter of a mile to walk. I was glad of a change although I was probably as bad as the rest of them for being impudent.

The teacher at the school I was to attend was a man; the first man teacher I had ever had. I didn't mind that part but he was in the process of being fired and was very nasty with the students. I had no quarrel with him but he sued the school district for his money and I was called as a witness. I was scared out of my wits. I had never been in a courtroom or seen a judge. You would have thought I was the one on trial. Anyway my father told me to tell them I had not been in school long enough to make a judgment so I was excused. He did eventually get his money.

A new teacher from Nebraska was hired and she "boarded" with us for the rest of the year. She was an excellent teacher and as there were just three of us in the eight grade, both of them two years older than I was, I made good progress. I think there were about eighteen or twenty altogether in all eight grades but she had taught in Idaho before and taught in rural schools where there were all eight grades so it was an easy task for her.

We had to go in to Blackfoot to the courthouse and take our final examinations given by the county superintendent. We were three scared girls as none of us had been around that many students before. All of Bingham County came there to take their exams. Surprisingly, we all made it.

As a final story, I went to Blackfoot high my freshman year and two months into my sophomore year; then we moved back to Mackay. By the time we were settled it was almost the first of February so I decided to skip it till the next year which I did. I stayed again with my grandparents and finished the next three years without a hitch, graduating just two months short of my eighteenth birthday.

Now for some of your other questions. What we wore? There were no slacks or snow boots but long-handled underwear with black stockings pulled up over the top and very hard to keep up. Usually ended up at the end of the day with many wrinkles. Our shoes were black laced and usually untied before long. We had probably two school dresses which we wore about a week. My hair was long and had to be braided before school. I think about seventh grade I was allowed one more dress as there was a church held in the building where I went to school. I would ride my horse to church and most of the time was invited to eat dinner with the minister and his family of about eight kids. That was the highlight of the week.

As for games, the kids played ball. We did what ever we could find to do until we got big enough that we were allowed to play baseball. Our ball was made of yarn unraveled from all the old worn-out men's wool socks. They didn't last very long. One of the girls mothers made them and the rests of us contributed socks. We played kick the can and some times hide and seek. In the spring it was marbles as soon as there was a bare spot. Sometimes in the winter if it was to cold to play outside the teacher would let us draw a ring on the floor with chalk and we could play marbles inside. We had chalkboards even in the very first school I went to. We just called them blackboards. Sometimes the teacher would let us play tic tac toe if we didn't get to noisy.

There were no cars in the country until I was about twelve years old and my folks didn't get one until many years after that. We went every place in a buggy with two horses hitched to it or my mother and I sometimes took a single buggy with one horse and go after the mail or groceries. My dad usually traded potatoes or grain at one store for the quantities of groceries like flour and sugar. Syrup in five gallon cans, crackers in big wooden boxes about the size of orange crates and several cans of coffee and other canned goods. We raised our own chickens and had our own eggs. We also raised pigs for bacon and sausage. We milked cows and had our own butter and cheese and made gallons of ice cream when we had snow or ice to freeze it with.

After I was about ten years old we got a telephone. There were about five in the little community. The poles were little cedar posts nailed on the fence posts and the farmers strung the wire and installed their own phones. Where the Post Office was they had the telegraph office and long distance telephone and I got to make a little money delivering messages to people who didn't have phones.

When I was eleven my dad bought cattle and it was my job to herd them in the summer time.

On weekends I would drive the sleigh team with a load of hay and help feed the cattle. That was about all the chores I had time to do as I had to leave for school about eight and didn't get home until about five. I had to take care of my own horse after I started riding to school.

Sometimes I would dry the supper dishes but usually I went to bed right after supper as I was rather a sleepy head.

One fun thing I would get to do even when I was quite small was go ice fishing with my dad and usually one of my uncles, either my dads brother or my mothers younger brother. My dad would hook one horse on a wooden box about four feet wide and eight feet long and drive the horse right out on the ice. They would cut a hole in the ice and pull the fish up through that hole. My mother usually sent a lot of hot rocks and blankets so I didn't get cold but it was a lot of fun.

I also had a swing in the shade of some big cottonwoods and I spent a lot of my time there. We had no close neighbors with small children so I pretty much had to entertain myself. I learned to keep time to music dancing with my doll while my dad played the violin. He was pretty strict about my keeping time because before he came West he used to call square dances and his sister and brother in law played the music. He has called as many as 20 sets; that is 160 people without a megaphone. He didn't stand for any foolishness.

So much for my growing up!

(NOTE: Mom had a handwritten note with this story that she had an electric typewriter and couldn't keep up with it! I left it pretty much as it was written by her with some corrections and deletions for brevity. I have tried to put a name on some of the rural schools she mentions from what I know about it. I can not guarantee that these will be correct. Stanley Potts, February 22, 2003. Feb. Twenty Second, Two Thousand and Three.)

This article appeared in the Idaho State University Outlook in the July-August, 1975, issue under the headline "Persistence Nets Diploma For Sarah Potts."

By Steve Guerber
ISU Outlook Editor

Sarah Gray Potts admits she's a persistent woman, although it may take her a little longer than normal to complete certain tasks.

When she entered Idaho Technical Institute in 1922, for example, she didn't even suspect the Pocatello school would undergo three name changes and a starting growth before she graduated in 1975.

"I only attended the school for nine weeks that first year before receiving a teaching certificate," she recalls. "I then left Pocatello and became a teacher at the old Franklin School in Custer County."

Located eight miles from Mackay near the Idaho Primitive Area, the one-room schoolhouse provided all the needs of area students in the first eight grades. Transportation for both pupil and teacher was by horseback in those days.

"Many times that winter my horse would get bogged down in the snow drifts while going to and from school," Sarah explains. "I'd have to get off and get the horse out of the drift before I could get going again. Sometimes I'd arrive at school wet from the waist down."

Perhaps such tribulations generated Sarah Potts' return to Idaho State for summer school and the winter semester of 1923-24 after one year at Franklin School. The following two years she was back in Custer County, however, this time at Alder Creek School, eight miles on the other side of Mackay.

After that she moved to Butte County and taught for two years at Cedarville School, located some 40 miles north of Arco between Clyde and Howe. Both of those two year periods(at Alder Creek and Cedarville) were again in one-room schools.

"It was 1928 when I was hired by the Forney school in Lemhi County," she remembers. "This was at only three pupils for that part of the year I was there."

Located on the South Fork of the Salmon River inside the primitive Area, the school was near Morgan Creek some 60 miles from Challis and 100 miles from Salmon.

"I began teaching school on January 6th, packing into the town during a lull in the weather. I never got back out until April 25th because of heavy snow that year," she explains. "The food we needed had been brought in by truck in the fall when roads were good and it lasted all winter."

Unmarried at the time, Sarah adds that there was "no use getting married. After all, there were four good looking men over there that winter."

Experiences in Forney proved in some cases to be something right out of the Old West one might expect to find in the primitive Area of Idaho, including at least one "gunfight."

"Actually, the boys were playing cops and robbers one day, only one of them had a loaded .22 pistol," she explains. "He accidentally shot one of the other boys."

Sarah Potts' efforts at first aid proved futile, however, as the victim died a short time later.

She left Forney to return to Alder Creek School, where she taught two more years in that one-room school before a move to the Pahsimeroi Valley near the Ima Mine. She was there for two years.

"One of my boys by the name of Joe Cockrell went on to become an outstanding student at the University of Washington and is now an electrical engineer," she recalls in reminiscing about children she had taught during her career. "The fact he was my most outstanding student during that period also proved to be a problem at one point."

"She explains: "Joe's father had told him that if he got straight A's he would given him a horse that he wanted. I knew of the promise, but I also knew if I gave Joe the A's early he wouldn't do anything in his studies – from then on and the rest of the kids in the class would follow his example. As a result, I did the only thing I could by waiting until the last week of school to give him his straight A's. and he did get the horse."

Sarah married a short time later, giving up the teaching profession until World War II created a shortage of teachers in 1945. Returning to Alder Creek to teach for two more years, she found the one-room school had grown to an enrollment of 26 students.

"I didn't completely overlook my education during those years I wasn't teaching, of course," Sarah reports. "I continued my learning at Idaho State during summer sessions and by taking continuing education courses offered by ISU at larger towns near where I worked and lived."

Between 1947 and 1951 she took time out to continue raising a family of her own, then went back to teaching at Mackay for a year. This time the school was a multi-room structure and here pupils were all in the second grade.

In, 1955 she went to the Little Lost River area and taught at the Clyde School for six years, returning periodically to Pocatello for summer school sessions.

"One winter I took a business law course while teaching at Clyde, driving into Arco for the classes," she remembers. "There were many nights that I didn't get home until the early daylight hours because of the snow and bad roads."

Sarah's daughter graduated from school in 1959 and went to a Ventura, Calif., college for a short time. She is now married to the manager of the Nugget Casino in Las Vegas.

Her son Charles graduated from high school in 1961 and from Idaho State in 1965 with honors. He is now writing books and preparing poetry and book reviews for a larger firm in Salt Lake City, where he also has his own band.

In 1961 Sarah Potts changed vocations when she and her husband began operating a grocery store at Hansen, near Twin Falls. She continued taking classes through ISU's continuing education program, however, completing her sophomore year of requirements with nine hours of credit received at Twin Falls and Kimberly class sessions.

In 1967, following a divorce from her husband, Sarah gave up the store at Hansen and moved to Nevada. She returned to teaching at the Fort McDermott Indian Reservation in Northern Nevada, guiding 17 Indians, one half-breed and a white youngster along the third grade program. "But the position lasted a mere 23 days because of a bureaucratic problem.

"The school found it couldn't give me a contract without a Nevada teaching certificate, but I couldn't get a certificate without a teaching contract, she explains.

The result was a move to O'Neil, a mid-point town between Wells and Jackpot in the Nevada desert. She was there for four years.

"Coyotes would keep you awake at night at O'Neil," she reports. "And unlike Hansen, where I had to sweep a few water snakes off the front porch of the grocery store, there were lots of rattlesnakes at O'Neil."

The O'Neil teaching job also brought some unusual mascots to one of Sarah's one-room school houses.

Included was a young cougar named 'Beelzebub."

"One of the families that lived near there also had raised an antelope on a bottle and she would come to school with the children in the morning, sleep on the door during the day, and return home with them when school was out," she says. Sarah still has a picture showing only "Suzie's" head peering at the camera the day snow covered her as it slept on the front steps of the school.

She left O'Neil in 1971 for a one year stint in Jiggs, 35 miles from Elko, then took her final teaching position in Jackpot, Nev..

"I went to summer school in 1969 and again in 1971 and 1973 I took classes in the ISU continuing education program at Twin Falls," she reports. The summer session of 1974 consisted of a 19-credit-hour effort which landed her on the Dean's list.

Sarah Potts' final session as an Idaho State student came last fall when, commuting from Jackpot to Twin Falls, she completed six hours of continuing education courses and wrote a term paper to meet final requirements for a bachelor of arts degree in elementary education.

During May 17 commencement exercises at Idaho State University, President William E. Davis halted ceremonies momentarily when Sarah Potts arrived at the podium to receive her diploma. Davis identified her as a woman who had been persistent enough to complete her degree requirements, although it took her 52 years to do so.

"The irony of the situation is the fact that the Jackpot School District decided to retire me now that I received my degree," adds Sarah, who will celebrate her 72nd birthday in late July. "I guess I'll just have to find something else to do now."

For Sarah Gray Potts, that comment may only be the beginning of another long career and attendance at a few more continuing education classes offered by Idaho State.

Mom was born July 14, 1903. Her One Hundredth Birthday would have been this July 14, 2003. The Lewis and Clark Expedition started out in 1803. The thesis mom wrote for her college graduation at age 72 was about their Voyage of Discovery and has a grade of A+. That sort of ties 200 years together, at least for this old scribe.

Chapter 1

Look Down On The Stars

Occasionally in traveling this rocky trail called life, we get to participate in a happening that smooths the bumps in the trail immensely.

One such happening occurred in the fall of 1983 on a sheep hunt in the Bighorn Crags of Idaho.

I had worked my way to the top of a high mountain near Wilson Peak just before dark

I moved rocks until I had a semi-smooth, level spot for my pad and sleeping bag. My plan was to be on this excellent vantage point in the morning so I could set up my spotting scope and scope for rams with the sun behind me. Hopefully, the rams would be moving around in some open country right after daylight.

Hunting had been very tough and I had been unable to locate a legal ram for my hunter, Roy Bridenbaugh. (See chapter 18 in *"The Potts Factor Versus Murphy's Law."* It is the diary of this 29-day hunt.) I thought the added advantage of being able to scope for several miles might allow me to locate a ram for him.

It was a clear night with no evidence of a storm so I just slept on top of the ground with no tent.

I woke up sometime in the middle of the night to one of the most spectacular views I have ever seen! The air was crystal clear and the millions of stars were glistening in all directions. The distant horizons were considerably below me in actuality but the impression of looking out at them in all directions was of being suspended in space and literally "Looking Down On The Stars!"

It was such a spectacular scene that I could not go back to sleep for several hours. My eyes just would not close to block out this magnificent event. I feel very privileged to have added this memorable scene to my memory bank of many "nights on the mountain!"

Incidentally, I didn't find any rams when morning came. I think my eyes were too tired from counting stars all night!

However, this spectacular panoramic view became the title for this, my second attempt to provide more insight into my life. Hope you enjoy it.

Chapter 2

Little Boy and Indians – The First Grade

I went to the first grade in three different schools, one in Mackay, Idaho, and the second two while Dad was working in the gold mine in Grass Valley, California.

While going to school in Mackay I had a couple of unique experiences with Indians. (As in Native Americans).

We lived two miles from Mackay and I rode the school bus. Somehow I missed the bus one afternoon, probably a marble game, and decided to walk home. About half way home and by Tom Pence's slaughterhouse I saw a team and wagon coming towards me. As it got closer I saw it was driven by an Indian with long braids and a big cowboy hat and with several other Indians in the wagon.

Stan Potts (far right) and the Evans' cousins at a picnic at Bear Creek about the time of the "Little Boy and Indians" story.

Being a little boy and having heard all kinds of kidnaping, scalping and Indian battle stories I went into a panic mode. I took off out through the sagebrush at a dead run and finally got far enough away that I felt safe and hid in the brush until they went by.

The Indians probably wondered what kind of weird wild kids were being raised in the Lost River country.

This was only two or three miles from where the Indians had ambushed and killed Jesse McCaleb and several other freighters as they were camped one night while hauling freight from Salmon to Mackay.

Dad had taken me to their grave site and told me the story. There were still people alive in the valley that were there when this happened so it was a story that was told quite often and made quite an impression on a little kid.

The reason the Indians were coming through from the reservation in Blackfoot was to go to the East Fork of the Salmon River to spear and dry Chinook salmon for winter's meat.

They would come through the valley going to the East Fork, stay up there until the salmon run was over and then return a month or so later to the reservation.

The second incident was only a few months after this Indian/wagon story.

The Indians would come up after deer season and trade gloves and moccasins for deer hides to tan and make more clothes.

They would camp down by the river with their teams/wagons/teepees for a month or so and then return once again to the reservation.

Dad took a load of deer hides over in our Model A Ford pickup to trade. While he was trading, the Indians would cut the scraps of meat from the hides and save them to cook or make jerky.

I was snooping around their camp and peeked into one of the tepees. There, laying on a tanned deerskin bed was a white woman!

Now, knowing very little about the ways of the world, I assumed she had been kidnaped. Right?

I kept trying to get Dad off away from the Indians so I could tell him and he could go rescue her.

When I was finally able to tell him he sort of explained she was probably there because she wanted to be.

A few years later I figured it out and was able to understand. She was probably just visiting and a friend of the Indians, or at least one of them!

Stanley Potts and paternal grandmother Ethel Coburn, about the time of the cotton fire.

Chapter 3

Little Boy and Fire

Like most little kids I had a fascination with fire. I had one experience that had the potential to rank right up there with the story of the lantern and Mrs. O'Leary's cow but somehow I lucked out.

The Lost River Valley floor was covered with cottonwood trees for many miles along the river where the water sub-irrigated out to give them moisture.

In early summer the trees would form the little cotton balls that opened up to fill the air and cover the ground with white cotton. Depending on the severity and timing of the spring frosts – some years there was no cotton – some years minimal cotton and some years it was like snow across the valley floor. It would plug your nostrils when you tried to breath and the wind would carry and drift it just like snow.

The near catastrophe I am about to relate was on one of the heavy cotton years, probably the worst I have ever seen. I was probably four or five years old – no matter – I was pretty young.

The ranch houses and homes along the valley south of Mackay were probably about one-quarter to one-half mile apart.

One of our closest neighbors Mel Hintze had a huge old two-story barn. He also had the only threshing machine in that end of the valley.

He would thresh his grain and blow the straw over the barn for insulation and handy bedding for the animals. He had cattle, hogs, chickens, turkeys, geese, ducks, sheep and horses.

The barnyard foul would scratch into the straw picking out grain that the threshing machine had missed and ended up making little trails in the straw, under the eves of the barn.

The birds then nested all over in their little hideout caves. Mrs. Hintze, Eulale, would hire me to find the nests and gather the eggs. I'd have done it for free just because it was such a neat place to play and explore. It was a small child's dream for a playground.

Back to the cotton. If you have never been around it, you probably won't understand what it is like with the cotton going into your nostrils with every breath. Each little wisp of the cotton has the little seeds to propagate the trees and they carry in the breeze for many miles.

I decided set it afire to see if it would burn. I guess it was just frustration from not being able to breathe.

In retrospect, I would been far better off to isolate a small amount of cotton for my experiment. I didn't, I just struck a match and held it to the cotton.

Unbeknownst to me, at that time, the cotton is mostly oil and volatile as gasoline!

Now visualize if you can, miles of cotton in all directions, laying and drifted against fences, homes, hay stacks, straw stacks and barns.

In a matter of a few seconds the cotton was burning in all directions and hundreds of yards away from me past and through our corrals and barns. It was headed through the trees to Mel Hintze's big straw stack, barn, corrals and home.

I was running along behind the flames crying – no idea what to do – even if I had been big enough to do anything. I was pretty sure that to just keep running and never come home would be my only chance of avoiding the beating I was going to get!

For whatever reason it didn't burn up the valley. As near as I can explain it would be like this. The cotton burnt so fast in most instances that it passed right over things with such speed that it didn't raise the temperature to the kindling point.

I remember stomping out a couple of small fires in dry leaves but by the time I had gotten to Hintzes, the fire was out.

Neighbors in other directions put out a few small fires but I guarantee you I learned what happens when you torch cotton!

My parents were so happy I hadn't destroyed the valley that all I got was a severe "talking to". Incidentally, that usually hurt worse and did more good than the old "razor strap" application!

Chapter 4

Trading Posts in Arizona

When I was in about the third or fourth grade I was lucky enough to spend a few weeks each summer for a couple of summers on the Navajo reservation in Arizona.

My Aunt Lemo Jarvis (my father's sister) ran trading posts for the Bureau of Indian Affairs at two different locations. One was "Tonalea" and the other was "Red Lake".

This was in the 1940's era and the Indians mostly still lived in hogans. The hogans are a type of house with curved walls and curved roof and constructed of poles and adobe mud. They would resemble an

A typical hogan.

igloo if made of ice. They were one room structures around twenty feet across with a small entrance about four feet high that was usually covered with a wool Navajo blanket or an animal hide. A hole in the center of the roof let the smoke out from a fire built on the ground, much like a tepee except permanent.

This served as each family's permanent home. Each family usually had a small herd of sheep and goats with a few families having some cattle also. Some of the family members lived a nomadic existence herding the animals out across the reservation to grass and water. They would return to their hogans with the animals several times a year. One return was in the spring to shear the sheep and goats.

The family members that stayed at the hogans raised gardens with lots of corn, maize and squash. They also cleaned and dyed the wool and mohair so the women could weave the beautiful Navajo rugs.

Some of the members also worked silver and turquoise into beautiful jewelry, concho belts, bracelets and squash blossom necklaces.

The Navajo rugs and silver and turquoise were the monetary basis of the Indian existence. Wealth was established by each family's herds of cattle, sheep, goats, horses, rugs, silver and turquoise jewelry.

Travel was by horseback or team and wagon. The trading posts served many purposes. They were the post offices, banks, pharmacies, grocery and department stores and rendezvous sites for the different families.

They may come for sixty miles or more with their teams and wagons which could be a three or four day trip each way. They would usually stay two or three days each trip and usually come twice a year.

The banking system was very unique with very little money used. It was primarily trading and pawn. As near as I can remember, here is how it worked.

The Indians would bring their trade goods-rugs and jewelry and exchange them for flour, sugar, salt, pepper, hats, shoes and cloth and velvet for clothes. If they needed money or didn't want to trade something right at that time, they would pawn it. The article would be held by the trading post for a period of time – say six months – and money or trade goods would be advanced. If the pawn was not redeemed then it could be sold by the trading post.

Now these trading posts were off the beaten path on dirt two track roads so the chance of being able to sell the rugs and silver at the trading post site was minimal. They had to be taken to some population center to be sold.

Flagstaff was the closest town and on the most major highway so that was where Lemo would take the trade goods and unredeemed pawn for sale.

The tourist trade as such had not come into being but the rugs and silver jewelry were being purchased as investments. Reputable dealers could sell the goods to galleries in New York or San Francisco over the phone with only the name of the artist or weaver and a description and dimensions of the work.

Each summer the town of Flagstaff had a big Indian celebration with parades, an Indian rodeo and Indian Powwow. This was the governmental meeting of the Indians-kind of like a legislature in session for a few days with the Navajo chieftan and his council making the reservation decisions for the coming year. At this time the old chieftan was Ataki Yazzi Begay.

This was one of the times Lemo would go to sell the rugs and jewelry and I got to go. She loaded her car, a big black four door sedan, with rugs and jewelry and we followed a two track road across the desert and up into the mountains to Flagstaff. The first paved road we hit was as we entered the city.

Finger painting of "Navajo John Lowe" by Lemo Vadis. Lemo Jarvis used the name "Lemo Vadis" for her art work.

It was a great get-together with some very talented Indian bronc riders and ropers competing in the rodeo. We stayed three or four days and then returned to the trading post.

Lemo was a frustrated artist like a lot of us but she did some beautiful finger paintings of the Indians, the desert and mountains and the Indian life.

The lake at Red Lake was dry most of the year. While walking out across it one day I found a petrified frog. Lemo said the frogs come up out of the dirt when the lake had water. This one turned into a little rock frog. Great summers for a little boy!

Chapter 5

**Billy Finley and the Roped Cow Fiasco
(Or, Not a Good Day To Go Fishing)**

When I was growing up in the Lost River Valley of the central Idaho mountains my parents had farms and ranches. We raised sheep, horses and cattle on the ranches and it seemed like we always had more livestock than feed for them so consequently my dad leased and rented pasture wherever he could find it.

The mining company (White Knob Copper Co.) had a section of land near the town of Mackay and at the end of railroad track where they had built their smelter. (Naturally, this was called the smelter field.)

The system of moving the ore from the mountain down to the smelter from the mine was a unique system and gravity powered. It consisted of an endless cable with huge ore buckets anchored to the cable every 100 yards or so. The cable ran through pulleys anchored near the top of giant wooden towers about fifty feet high and designed in such a manner that the full ore buckets pulled the empty buckets back up the mountain.

The full ore buckets containing a ton or two of copper ore came down the mountain, probably a couple miles. The elevation drop was somewhere around 2,000 to 2,500 vertical feet.

As the weight of the ore in the full buckets coupled with the force of gravity descended, the empty buckets were pulled back up to the headhouse. The distance between the buckets was exact so that as the full bucket was dumping at the smelter at the bottom of the mountain an empty bucket was being filled from the ore chute at the headhouse at the top of the mountain. It was an endless journey engineered so that it was powered only by gravity.

Anyway, back to the story about Billy Finley and the cow. The Big Lost River ran by the smelter and the mill used water from the river in the smelting process. The mill complex probably sat on twenty or so acres of the 640 and the balance of the land was fenced – with the river meandering through it. The ground was covered with big willow, cottonwood, quaking aspen and sagebrush but with good grass underneath. The west, upriver end of the field was only one half mile or so from the village of Mackay.

There were many great fly fisherman in Mackay and Billy Finley was one of them. He probably stood 5'4" and weighed in at seven stone and some change with his hip boots full of water!

Now Billy and the other fly fisherman would walk down the smelter road or along the railroad tracks toward the trestle and cut through the field and through the brush to their favorite water.

On this particular day Billy's timing was not good.

We had a sick cow that dad wanted me to find, rope and doctor. What the cow's ailment was I don't remember, but once again a chance to practice my roping was looked upon as nearly a vacation from regular ranch work (fence building and haying).

Finding an individual animal in one square mile of brush takes a while so it was late afternoon when I located the cow. You just don't build a loop in your rope and race through the jungle chasing the cow. There is a certain amount of subterfuge and guile involved to get the proper throw between trees and brush. Consequently, you casually follow the cow around with the rope and loops hidden or at least not in plain sight until you see a small opening ahead of you where you can spur your horse ahead, get the cow into one of the small openings, take a swing and place the rope over her head and get your dallies before you get dragged off by a limb or tree.

I did all of the above with ridiculous ease – got my horse stopped and my dallies on the horn. The cow went left around a big willow and thereby hangs the tale. "Tail?"

Poor Billy was ambling through the brush – not a care in the world, dreams of eight pound rainbows no doubt in his mind – when all of a sudden he is tied to a willow by a lariat rope with a mad cow on one end and a horse and kid on the other!

I got around the willow, which was probably twenty feet across, and saw the predicament with poor Billy upside down and the cow right by him and definitely on the fight.

I dropped my dallies so the cow could leave and got off to help poor Billy assess the damage.

Other than a few bruises and some scattered fishing gear he came out of it reasonably well and went on his way toward the river. I doubt if his casts were of their normal beauty the rest of the day. It's hard to cast looking over your shoulder!

I finally followed the cow around till I picked up my rope – got her doctored and rode then home to tell my story.

Chapter 6

The Lightning Strikes

I've heard that some people attract lightning. I don't know if I'm one of those or if it is true or not. All I know is I've had a few calls somewhat closer than I enjoyed.

I've seen first hand what lightning can do. The most memorable was a lightning strike in cottonwood trees that killed five of our milk cows that were bedded near the base of a tree.

My first close call was when I was seven or eight years old. I was riding my mare, Spider, that my brother had given me when he joined the Navy prior to the Second World War.

I had ridden her out into the Burnett Ditch, a large irrigation canal, and she had her head down getting a drink of water. It had just started to rain lightly. There was a loud crack as a lightning bolt hit very close by. Spider dropped to her knees in the water and then stood back up. The saddle I was riding had a brass horn and it was actually warm when I touched it. I think the lightning must have hit right behind us as I never saw any flash of light.

I second near miss was only a couple years later. Dad and I were gathering cattle to move them from the low mountains where our BLM permit was up on the national forest. I think that was usually about the first of June, so that is the approximate time of year.

We were riding about thirty feet apart and going around a hillside that rose above my left side. It started to rain and hail with scattered lightning strikes in the vicinity. All of a sudden about ten feet from me and about my eye level the lightning hit! It was an experience I will never forget and I have never heard lightning strikes explained anywhere near what I saw.

The bolt that hit the ground was not jagged like the pictures and cartoons. It was a perfectly round orange ball, probably eighteen inches in diameter. Above and to the side and connected to it by orange rods were about four or five smaller balls. I'd like to call them balls of fire but that's not what it was like. They were more like molten lava, but perfectly round and the connecting rods perfectly round. The smaller orbs were probably four to six feet from the larger one.

Keep in mind that this was probably a millisecond in time but I happened to be looking in the right direction.

My horse fell away from me and down the mountain towards Dad. I ran towards her and she got up immediately with no evidence of being hurt. As I got back on dad hollered "Let's get the hell out of here." I tell you, if he was waiting on me he was killing time!

My third close call was a couple years after that and there were four of us involved this time. My high school coach, Nolan Sayer, was a rancher also and I was working for him and his brother, Treasure, one summer stacking bales of hay.

We were in a field north of the railroad tracks loading bales on a wagon pulled by an old jeep when it started to rain. We crawled under the wagon for a few minutes but it started raining real hard and we knew we couldn't load any more bales 'till they dried out. We decided to head for the house. Now, when we got to the railroad tracks there was a gate to open.

The other person helping us was John Pilash. John was somewhat mentally impaired. The story I remember was that his mother had gotten smallpox while she was carrying him and had a very high fever which caused him brain damage. He was a big stout guy and a great worker.

Nolan put his irrigating boots on and got his shovel out the Jeep. He was going to change the floodwater on his field peas.

Treasure was driving the Jeep. John was opening the gate, and Nolan was stepping over a barb wire fence to get to his water set.

I was sitting in the back of the jeep, facing forward when once again a giant CRACK!

I saw Nolan fly in the air still hanging on the top wire. Treasure dived out of the Jeep face down in the dirt. (This was right after World War II and Treasure had evidently been shell-shocked during the war). John dropped the gate and started running down the railroad track.

This all happened in a short second or so and I felt or saw nothing except my partner's actions and airtime.

When we got everybody back at the jeep and were all okay, we looked for the strike. It had hit a bale of hay about six feet behind the Jeep and just exploded it. We used wire balers and the wire had burned off the top side of the bale. The ends where they had touched the ground were melted into little round balls of metal and holes about six inches deep were in the ground where the lightning had grounded.

Those are the most memorable "near misses"! There have been many more of lesser excitement.

It is true that you can feel your hair stand up on the back of your neck prior to a lightning storm but there is not much you can do about it except to talk to the guy upstairs and try to convince him that you're sorry for all those bad things you have done and promise to do better in the future!

1900 - Home in the old abandoned town of CLIFF, Idaho (Located in Cliff Creek) Ada Evans Gray and Herb Gray

My maternal grandparents, Ada Evans Gray and Herbert Martin Gray, in a photo taken in 1901 at the town of Cliff west of Mackay. Photo courtesy Joe Ausich.

Chapter 7

Tommy Ding

Every community has its characters. Some of us, I mean some of them, are a little more memorable than others.

When I was growing up in the Lost River Valley of Idaho there lived in the mountains to the southwest of the town of Mackay a very memorable one. His name was Thomas F. Bennett, but the local populace had somehow bestowed upon him the moniker, "Tommy Ding".

Tommy Ding (at left) and Dave Bell in a photo taken in 1961. Photo courtesy Joe Ausich.

Tommy, according to the local lore, was from England and had graduated from Oxford. His handwriting was probably the most beautiful I have ever seen.

Tommy was a prospector-miner-hermit and a bit of a drinking man. He had mining claims scattered throughout the White Knob mountains. The claims were marked with monuments, usually wooden posts set in the ground, with Prince Albert tobacco cans nailed to the posts.

Inside the cans were a description of each claim's dimensions with natural monuments, trees, streams, rocks etc. and directions from same explaining the claim perimeters.

We ran cattle through those mountains and whenever I was near one of Tommy's cabins, I would stop and visit. When I found one of his claim markers I would open the Prince Albert can and read the claim notice just to look at his beautiful handwriting. I don't know what his writing was called but it was an artistic, flowery scroll.

Tommy had summer and winter cabins and I guess picked them for sun exposure – distance to firewood and water, and distance to the claims he was working, etc. He also, obviously, picked them by the necessity of their being abandoned by the previous inhabitant.

One of the cabins had probably been abandoned by some "older timer" many years before and sort of "reclaimed" by Tommy. The cabin was probably 14'x16' with a dirt roof. The weight of the dirt had sagged the poles holding the roof and Tommy or someone had reinforced the system with upright posts in the necessary spots. Unfortunately, the necessary spots were about every three or four feet. There was a wood stove, table and chairs and bed that I remember plus some storage boxes. Quarters could possibly be explained as "tight". Turning edgewise was necessary in some spots to get between the posts.

Now Tommy would usually come to town a few times each year to get groceries and see the bright lights with an occasional, no usual, meeting with the "Demon Run" worked in. Tommy usually was accompanied by some type of "Hienz 57" type canine.

After one of Tommy's parties at the local "Gin Clinics" he had gone into Tom Pence's market for his groceries still "three sheets to the wind" so to speak. (He'd probably spent all of his money and planned on talking Tom into some credit).

Evidently Tom's patience had worn thin. I was probably five or six years old and we were parked in front of the store. I could hear a noisy commotion inside.

Shortly thereafter the screen door flew open and Tommy Ding came flying out into the sidewalk, propelled by Tom Pence's foot. Tommy D. bounced to a halt on the sidewalk, the door slammed shut, and a few seconds later the same scenario with a big yellow dog being the recipient of the "foot propulsion"!

I'm not sure what store he got his supplies from but I doubt it was the Pence Market on that trip.

Tom Pence worried about the old guy, right along with the rest of the town and valley inhabitants.

Tommy Ding would usually come out around February and if he didn't there would be some type of "take some supplies and check on Tommy trip organized."

It usually would entail four or five guys with horses to go as high up the mountain as possible and then ski or snowshoe on up. The horses could usually go three or four miles depending on snow depth, with another two or three on foot. Every trip started out with the worry that Tommy had expired. But, "We better take him some groceries just in case."

When whoever got there first he would usually be greeted with, "What are you guys doing? Figured I'd died, I bet!"

The groceries and small flask of John Barley Corn were the back-up and "No! We figured you could use some fresh groceries" would save the day.

Oh, by the way. Tom Pence was usually on those trips along with Carl Wall, Leonard Wall, Vivian Wornek, Verl Potts and others. I made a couple of trips myself.

Chapter 8

Mistaken Identities and Mining at Cobalt

With the name "Stanley Potts" you would think you would be fairly free from being plagued with a multitude of Stanley Pottses in the world! However, that isn't so and whether the "Potts Factor" comes into play here I'm not sure!

My daughter, Kay, getting a bath in the kitchen sink in one of the "lambing sheds" while we were mining at Cobalt. April, 1955.

Anyway, when I first started working in the mine at Cobalt was my first encounter with the problem.

I had worked there a month or so and Joy had brought our baby daughter Kay up over the snow covered mountain pass, (Morgan Creek Summit) in our old Buick Car to be with me. We lived for a while with my Dad's cousin, Buck Allen, and his wife until we could get an apartment. The apartments (little duplex cabins) were referred to by the tenants as "the lambing sheds."

Payday was every two weeks and the mine owned the "lambing sheds" and the grocery store. In order to survive between paychecks you could draw a book of vouchers to buy groceries. The rent was deducted from your paycheck along with the vouchers you had purchased. Now at $1.64 an hour even with all the overtime and contracting money I could get, the checks were pretty small.

I was only twenty years old when the first and most major "mistaken identity" came into being. The first I became aware of it was a registered letter from the Internal Revenue Service stating that I owed several thousand dollars in back income tax and that they would be attaching my petty pay check to apply to the tax.

Next, Idaho Power, the same thing – a registered letter wanting huge amounts of money to pay my power bill at the "Pheasant Grill" in a town in Oregon. I think it was Burns or Bend.

I politely wrote them informing them I was only twenty years old, had never been to Oregon and had never earned a fraction of the money I supposedly owed the IRS or Idaho Power. Then more letters from a sheriff in Oregon – Child abandonment – Back rent – you name it. All my spare time was spent trying to tell these people I wasn't their man (or boy?)

Idaho Power especially could not be convinced. I finally wrote them and informed them that if they kept pressing it I was fairly confident that I would own Idaho Power at the finish of the proceedings!

That must have got someone's attention and everyone quit hounding me for some other "Stanley Potts" problems.

An interesting side note here. Six or seven years after this when we were ranching in Nevada, I received a letter from a "Patsey Potts" in Oregon. I opened it and it started off :Dear Sir; I am wondering if you may be my father?

This girl had seen my name in some rodeoing publications and was still searching for the father that had abandoned her many years before.

Obviously – bad as I am – I'm not the worst "Stanley Potts" of all time!

In recent history there has been another play on the name. There is another Stanley Potts in the Midwest who is a fairly famous writer, hunter and evidently TV personality. I have sold several copies of my first book, *"The Potts' Factor Versus Murphy's Law,"* to people that wrote and said "I have seen you on television and want to buy your latest book! I was glad to oblige and didn't inform them that my "latest book" was also my "firstest book"!

Mining At Cobalt

This is a good place to add some of my mining experiences of which there have been many! Underground miners especially become a little weird after living like moles for a lengthy period of time.

When I went to work at the Blackbird Mine in Cobalt, I noticed these guys playing tricks on each other – on the bus to the mine, in the lunchroom and underground etc. At first I was rock solid and nothing bothered me, but after a few months of watching their tricks on each other – some of them pretty wild – I began moving around while looking over my shoulder also. I'll list some of the more memorable pranks.

There was young miner, maybe even younger than me, named "Cougar Roy". I have no idea what his last name was but he had been raised in the mountains. Someone had a clipping from the Salmon paper with him standing looking up at a street light. He was a teenager and that evidently had been his first trip to town.

The nickname "Cougar Roy" had been bestowed on him for the following reason. In recent years, a host of new laws restricting methods of hunting mountain lions had been put in place across the west. In other words: no dogs, no trapping, etc. Some people have been occasionally successful in finding a fresh track and following it long enough to force the cougar to climb a tree to keep from being harassed.

The story on Cougar Roy was that he had done this about sixteen times already in his life! I have no idea but here is the rest of the story on my involvement with him.

He was a tall, husky, good-looking, blond, elderly kid. Being raised alone, evidently, he had never had anyone to play with in any manner including wrestling, rough housing etc.

I was the closest in size and age to Roy of the miners that rode this particular bus up the mountain and back from work each day.

The other miners must have gotten their heads together and decided it would be fun to see Roy and Stan in some type of physical altercation.

Their plan was fairly simple. Each one of us packed a black lunch bucket with Thermos®. The mine worked three shifts and everyone revolved so you may be getting on the bus in the middle of the night and looking forward to your "spamburger" and coffee at three or four in the morning.

When you got on the bus, you placed the lunch bucket under your seat to be taken off when the bus got to the mine.

We pretty much all sat in our favorite seats on the bus. Mine was near the front and Roy's was near the back.

The miners must have been all in on this one as they somehow were able to slide Roy's lunch bucket with their feet all the way from the rear of the bus to the front and guess what seat it ended up under?

Right, poor Potts! When Roy noticed his lunch bucket was gone he started looking for it. Now, I, not having a clue what was transpiring, was sitting there fat dumb and happy and oblivious to the miners keeping track of what would shortly transpire.

When Roy spotted the lunch bucket, he was standing in the aisle right by my seat and looking at me with a pretty piercing stare. I looked down and there was his lunch bucket under my seat. About then the bus exploded in laughter and Roy tackled me.

The look on his face was not so much in anger but more like, "Hey, I'll politely teach this guy a lesson." He wasn't swinging at me but more wrestling with me. As I said, he was my size and fast and strong and we were in the aisle, over other seats and mashing other people. Every time I could see his face it was like a partial grin and he was having the time of his life. "At last I get to play!"

I, on the other hand, had played before, and this was about as rough a type of play as I had ever been involved in. Finally, the bus got to the parking lot at the mine and our wrestling match ended. The miners had succeeded in releasing their boredom once again!

Also riding the bus was a white Russian named Nicolia Chukov. Nicolia murdered the King's English very well. He knew all the cuss words with miner's vocabulary, but his syntax was out of order. It was "Son of a bitch – you god dam" etc.

Nicolia was our "nipper". Hauled supplies (dynamite, caps, primer cord, fuse, drill bits, etc) on a little electric train and delivered them to each stope, drift, raise etc.

He would usually hit one of the lunchrooms at lunchtime as they were heated with wooden benches and electric lights. One of the lunchrooms was on a big curve in the train track. One of the miners hooked a long log chain to the last car on Nicholia's train with plenty of slack so he could pick up speed when he started.

When he started out – got it moving pretty good on the curve – the chain came tight and jerked all his cars and electric engine (power unit) called a "manshee" off the track. The inverted cuss words, when he found out what happened, filled the air in all directions!

He was not the cleanest person that ever lived. (As in B.O.) It hovered near him at all times. The miners played a big trick on him that backfired. They got his hard hat, a necessary piece of equipment, and rubbed limburger cheese inside the sweatband so that when it warmed up it would smell worse than horrible! Guess what? Nicolia never even knew about it, but it drove the rest of us far away.

Another time – the lunch bucket trick with a major refinement. They got his lunch bucket – placed some taped together flares inside it (they look a lot like dynamite sticks) and connected primer cord to the flares, leaving a foot or so sticking out to light a match to it at the proper time.

They got it back under his seat and someone casually lit the primer cord. Nicolia smelled it burning, saw smoke coming out of his lunch bucket lid – opened the lid and here was the dynamite (flares really), ready to blow. He threw it clear to the back of the bus and was trying to get out of the bus but the driver who was in on the trick – wouldn't open the door!

More inverted cuss words – believe me!

Another wild one. There was a Spaniard named Joe Unamuno who spoke no or very little English. Rumor had it that he was the heavyweight champion boxer of Spain who had ended up in the United States after a fight and became a miner. I don't not know but he was big, strong, active and I didn't want to play with him – actually avoided him all I could.

I signed up for all the overtime I could, as we needed every penny we could get. I signed up for clearing track with a mucking machine one Sunday. Guess who my partner was? Yup. Joe Unamuno.

Because of his size and demeanor (as in big and tough) he pretty well controlled all activity near him. We were working our way along a drift, clearing the drain ditch with shovels and loading the ore car behind the mucking machine. When I evidently did something that did not meet with Unamuno's approval, he grabbed me to reiterate his displeasure and I reacted out of impulse.

Remember, the only light was from a light on each of our hard hats powered by a battery on our belts. The batteries were charged after each shift. You turned your head to where you needed light.

When he grabbed me I immediately turned my light to his head and instinctively and probably stupidly laid a right hand on his jaw with all my might! If I had thought this out I guarantee this never would have happened, but for once in my life impulse worked successfully.

Unamuno's hard-hat and light went crashing one way and he bounced off the rocks the other. I thought then for the first time, "I'm dead".

However, Joe got up, got his hat and light and we went back to work. From then on we became the best of friends. His reason I'm not sure of, but mine was I'd surely rather be his friend instead of his enemy!

He, through the few words of English he could speak and write offered me $200.00 if I could get him a job in a mine in Utah. He wanted me to write them with a recommendation on his abilities. Probably be called a resume nowadays.

Anyway, I wrote it for him but the mine at Cobalt went on strike and I never went back when it reopened several months later. I don't know if Joe got his job or not.

Probably the next best-worst story involved our shift boss, Arnold Castle, and the foreman, Jim Salyers.

Arnold's brother, Walt, was my partner and taught me most of what I know about the mining game.

These two weren't above playing games themselves and this one got someone even.

They were constantly going around the mine to different levels to check on progress, safety procedures, following ore veins, etc. Because of the size and complexity of the operation they may only make an individual operation every week or so. They had both been in the mining field for a long time, had seen and had tricks played on them before and had played many tricks of their own. A couple of the stope miners went to great lengths on this one.

The mine was one large rumor mill but fairly accurate as to what was happening on each level (elevation) and the time of the boss' visit could be guessed at fairly closely. You told where you were working by elevations – "I'm stoping on the 7,100, 7,400 level, etc."

These two miners found a couple of the most ghastly rubber pullover Halloween masks that you could imagine, along with a couple of deformed hands with claws and with all fluorescent colors.

When the bosses come up the ladder into the stope these guys were all suited up and ready – running the drills on the jack legs and drilling away at the face with their masks and hard hats on. Remember the only light is on the hard hats.

Well, the bosses come up and tapped these miners on the back. The miners turned around and the bosses light shown on the hideous pair with huge, bloody, fluorescent scars and gleaming off center eyes!

There were lots of stories as to what happened next – from Castle and Salyers both passing out from fright to them going back down the ladder with great haste and only stepping on about every sixth rung.

One of the miners named Kooni stuttered quite badly and when he tried to talk fast it was worse. He was walking down the drift one shift and one of his "friends," none other than Arnold Castle wrapped up in burlap that was used in the sand fill operation and hid under an ore chute; when the miner walked by, Castle jumped out and roared like a bear!

The poor stuttering Kooni raced down the drift and tried to tell everyone he saw what happened. All he could get out was "oye oh and ond and she she went woof woof!"

(An interesting sub-note here on Kooni's idea of elk meat, courtesy of Buck Allen.) Buck said that he, Bill O'Neal and Kooni had driven up the mountain road out of Cobalt to see if they could find an elk to shoot. The weather turned to snow and they decided to abandon the hunt, turned around and headed home. Kooni said that is lucky because you can't eat elk meat anyway.

He asked them if they knew what compared to good elk meat and then proceeded to tell them. He said, "First, you go find a poor old Holstein cow, starve her down for a few more days, then run her around for a couple hours until her tongue is hanging out about a foot. Then you shoot her, making sure you don't do a clean job of it. Wait several hours or up to a few days before you dress her out. Hang the carcass up for several days, preferably in a warm building; before you cut it up. Now, you have good elk meat."

That is when they realized that Kooni did not like elk meat!

The miners all had some kind of story about tough drilling conditions/ hard rock etc.

One lunch break the stories about hard rock were making the rounds – having to go after more bits in the middle of the shift, only getting one eight-foot hole in a full shift, etc.

One grizzled old miner stopped the stories with, "Hell, kids you don't know what hard rock is? I drilled six hours, used all my bits and had to hold my finger on the spot while my partner went after more bits!" He was the hard rock winner of those stories!

I'll end the Cobalt mining stories with this one. There was one miner that never rode the bus. He had a pretty black sedan and drove it up the hill to work every day, always by himself. He could leave twenty minutes or so after the bus and be to work on time.

One day I missed the bus and was standing on the corner hoping someone would come by and give me a ride. This guy came by and stopped and I caught a ride. On the seat was a large pistol and standing up from the floorboard was a large rifle, which I perceived as somewhat odd. There weren't any hunting seasons on.

A couple nights later I found out why he drove. He would wait until the bus picked up a certain miner and then would stop by and visit the miner's wife. They were probably old friends or something. Anyway, this miner had found out about the visits, there was a miner gunfight and the black car left for other pastures.

A high percentage of my friends in the mining business were killed in different mine accidents in the next few years. Three of them in the fire at the Lucky Friday mine in northern Idaho. It's a dangerous business and that's probably why they work some levity into their existence.

Chapter 9

Highway Patrolman Stories

I have a unique knack for running afoul of the law, with Highway Patrolman, especially. Sometimes their rules and my system just don't mesh.

I'll chronologically go through some of my most memorable lash-ups.

One year when I lived in Mackay, my neighbor and team-roping partner, Owen Brabb, and I were going on a sheep buying trip to southern Idaho and Wyoming. He had a big Buick Century Sedan and I was driving. This was about 1955 and the speedometer was broken on the car.

We had several opportunities to look at sheep on this trip and the first one was in Twin Falls, Idaho. We were running a little late as we turned south at Shoshone, about twenty miles north of Twin Falls..

I came over a hill and there was a patrolman headed South ahead of us. It seemed like he was going awfully slow.

Brabb and I talked it over and decided I would slowly pass him – slowly ease away and when we got out of sight we would let her roll again.

The first couple of things worked okay. We slowly passed – slowly eased away, just about out of sight and ready to "let her roll" when here he came, the red lights flashing.

I pulled over and two of the biggest patrolmen I have ever seen got out and come to both sides of the car.

I rolled down the window and was looking somewhere between my guys knees and his belt buckle! I gave my plea for leniency. We were visiting, didn't realize we were a little too fast, etc. He didn't give me a ticket, but pulled in front of me and believe me, I didn't pass him again although I'm sure he was only doing about 50!

Port of Entry Lash Ups

When Joy and I bought the ranch in Clover Valley, Nevada, we had a station wagon and horse trailer, a ton and a half truck and a pickup to take from Idaho. They had all just been licensed in Idaho in January and we moved in March. There was a Port of Entry in Wells and the Captain in charge knew all about us. His name was Bernard Bartz, "Barney" to the locals.

Barney informed me that all the rigs would have to be relicensed in Nevada even though they had new Idaho licenses. I went to the County Seat, Elko, to get the new licenses. The county assessor, Evo Granata, told me that no, Nevada and Idaho had a reciprocity agreement and I would not have to relicense until they expired in Idaho.

I returned to Wells and informed "Barney" of what I had found out. To say the very least, he was not thrilled with my findings of his not knowing the law and this started my "port of entry" problems.

When I was rodeoing, I pulled my dogging horse, Brandy, that I had gotten from Harry Charters in a one-horse trailer behind our old Buick. Harry had gotten Brandy from world champion cowboy Dean Oliver. She had been Dean's first calf roping horse and became like one of our family.

I had a brand inspection card that was like an unlimited trip permit as long as the same rig, driver, horse, etc, was involved.

I came into the port of entry at Hollister, Idaho, about midnight one night and the patrolman on duty wouldn't honor my permit. He told me I'd have to go back to Twin Falls and get a current brand inspection. I argued to no avail so turned around and went back about twenty miles to Twin Falls to the stockyards, hoping there would be a brand inspector around. Slim chance at one o'clock in the morning. Sure enough there wasn't one.

I got on the phone and finally got a hold of the Lincoln County Sheriff, Wid Conner, who was the brand inspector also and had given me the trip permit. He was not in a very good mood from being aroused from a sound sleep anyway. He said, "I'll call that dumb #@*! And tell him what the law is!"

He did and I returned to the port of entry. Another one of those deals that doesn't make you any points, however, and you better be right the next time through!

Sure enough more problems. We were in a bad drought in Nevada and hauling hay from Howe, Idaho. My neighbor, Vernon Dalton, and I had bought hay and another neighbor, Darrell Weeks, was helping us haul. We had two ton and a half bob tails with overshots, one with a trailer, and Dalton's semi.

The port of entry people were not all that thrilled with our little convoy, anyway, especially after being put down with the brand inspection deal.

We set an all time record on one trip. There were three major ways to be in violation of the rules – overweight, over-width, and over-height. Guess what, they got us for all three – one for each truck!

The judge was back up the road about a half a mile in the little town of Hollister. His name was Judge Henstock and he ran the gas station and grocery store also.

The port of entry loaned us their police cruiser to go back and pay our fines!

I was a little flustered when we came up in front of the Judge and mispronounced his name pretty badly. In my usual plea for leniency I said, "We're sorry, Judge Hunsucker!" In retrospect, my mis-saying of his name probably didn't cut us any slack in the fine!

A funny (for some) thing happened about that time by the cemetery just out of Carey, Idaho. It started out with a flat tire on my truck.

I'd pulled over, had jacked the truck up and was changing the tire when about a thousand or so sheep came over the hill, being driven by several men. The sheep herders and dogs were moving them up the road and they were about half past my truck, going around on both sides. All of a sudden, one of the tires on the other side of the truck blew out with a giant BANG!

The sheep herd immediately panicked, stampeded, tore the fences down on both sides of the highway and scattered in all directions!

It's a good thing I don't speak Spanish or Basque because I think I might have been mentioned in some of the words emanating from the "mutton conductors" as they rounded up their panicked charges! My daughter, Stani Malmgren, and her husband Chris live right by there now (2002). When I'm at their house and look down at the highway I still relive that wild morning.

One spring as I was getting ready to go to the rodeo in Battle Mountain, I realized my horse trailer license was expired. I figured I'd stop in Elko and get it renewed but forgot it was Saturday and they were closed.

The Elko County brand inspector, Tom Kane, came out of his office at the courthouse and I explained my dilemma. He suggested I tack a gunnysack over the license where it would be hard to read and go on. I decided that would just draw attention to it so I'd go ahead and explain my problem if I got stopped.

As I was going through Elko, a patrolman pulled in behind me at the Commercial hotel intersection and followed me about 15 miles, nearly to Carlin. Then the red lights went to blinking and I pulled over. I gave him my story and in the course of explaining that I "was going to get a new license in Elko" he very smartly explained "You belong to the 'I was gonna club' don't you?" and started writing out the ticket.

Me, not being in a great mood at this point in time anyway, decided there was no sense in hauling an expired license plate around.

I took it off of the trailer as he was writing the ticket and sailed it into the wind like a saucer. Got a great angle on it and it went clear across the railroad tracks, probably over 100 yards.

As he was finishing the ticket he said "What was the number on that license?" My reply, "you saw where it landed. I don't know."

He crawled through the two barbed wire fences-both directions-and tore his gabardine breeches on a barb. Now, NEITHER of us were in great moods at this juncture in time when who should drive up but Tom Kane, who also was headed for the rodeo.

Poor Tom, not having any idea of what had recently transpired was going to help me talk this guy out of the ticket!

Alas, Tom had arrived far too late for that, but I sure appreciated the attempt.

Sheep Hunt Speeding Ticket

We had a big blue International TravelAll. The kids called it the tank, as it was nearly bomb proof. They loved it because they could get nearly half the kids in school in it to drag main, attend school functions, go to band and cheerleading practice, etc.

Two of my friends, Dick Hall and Bob Queroz, had drawn Desert Bighorn sheep tags on the bombing range near Indian Springs out of Las Vegas, Nevada.

I took the tank and went down to help them look for sheep. We had to attend two different indoctrination schools – one from the Air Force on unexploded ordinance (hot bombs and rockets) laying around, and one from the Nevada Department of Wildlife on legal-sublegal sheep.

The hunt was over the Christmas-New Years vacation period and ordinarily there was no training going on with jet fighter planes from the air base at Indian Springs practicing air to air combat and making practice bombing runs.

However, the Vietnam War had gotten underway and the Air Force was training South Vietnamese pilots during this time. The Air Force gave us the hot areas to stay out of and to keep someone from getting hurt.

We had a small camp trailer and went into the west side of the Pintwater range up toward Quartz Springs and set up camp.

The season was supposed to be two weeks long. We hunted the first day splitting up with me in the middle so I could signal Dick or Bob if I saw anything.

We didn't find anything and met back at our trailer. The next day we did the same thing, hiking up a different stretch of mountain. During the day I noticed what seemed an inordinate amount of traffic out in the valley between the Pintwater range and the Spotted Range. Lots of dust – rigs with red lights, etc.

I found a couple of good rams and signaled Dick onto them. I watched through the spotting scope as he made the stalk, up to what I guessed eighty to one hundred yards and the rams ran off without a shot. When Dick and I got together I asked him why he didn't shoot. He replied, "I thought there might be a bigger one." I asked what he thought the best one would have scored. He said, "about 160."

Now, during the Department of Wildlife school you had to guess sheep scores and age them through a spotting scope. Dick had been consistently eight to ten points less on his guesses than the actual score. I had guessed the best one at 168. Anyway, we watched a big ram run up the mountain.

That evening when we got back to our trailer camp there was a large (as in about 2'x 3' sign) on the door. It was hand written in red marker and said "BY ORDER OF COMMANDER_____. THIS AREA IS TO BE EVACUATED IMMEDIATELY!" Now, desert sheep tags are a prized possession. People have tried to draw one for a lifetime and not been able to. We had no idea who was going on, but Dick said: "They aren't gong to get me out of here before I get my ram". He started repacking his pack frame, getting extra water and food, etc. He was nearly done when we heard a vehicle coming up our little two track road very speedily.

We stepped out to be greeted by a couple of large-bodied, black air patrolman and they told us, "Hook on to the trailer gentlemen, and follow us."

They didn't know exactly what had happened but rumor had it that someone had parked a vehicle in one of the hot areas and a South Vietnamese pilot had made a strafing run on it. The Air Force commander was removing everyone. So, we followed them out. We got back to the Indian Springs Air Force Complex and were checked out. We then went on to the Corn Creek sheep station, where all the sheep hunters were at Dr. Charles Hansen's house trying to get some answers as to what to do. He was in charge of the wildlife there for the Nevada Department of Wildlife and also I think the U.S. Fish and Wildlife Service. This was about 1:00 o'clock in the morning.

Guide Dick Hall and big desert ram.

The best he could explain it was the Commander had effectively closed the sheep hunt in the bombing range and would not be changing his mind.

The seventeen-member Nevada Fish and Game Commission would be holding a conference call as soon as they could all be contacted and available.

(Ultimately two or three days later. They opted to open all sheep areas in Nevada to these seven tag holders.)

I was unable to stay, but Dick and Bob went to the sheep range and the desert range. They both got rams with Dick's getting the award for the best Trophy Score in Nevada that year. Trophy score is the score of the best horn doubled. One horn was broken off about 10"/12". The Trophy Score was about 171. Anyway, a great ram for a great guy. Dick died of a brain tumor not too many years later. He was one of my best friends. Also, Dr. Hansen was killed in a tragic helicopter crash in Utah a short time after this.

Back to the Highway Patrolman story. This is why some people like my stories.

I can start out telling about a hangnail and work in the History of Mankind before it is over!

The tank was not a real speedwagon. It's uphill most of the way from Las Vegas to Wells. I had driven as fast as it would go all the way to the pass south of Ely and not gotten over about sixty. There was no speed limit then. I think it was something like, "reasonable and prudent!" I headed down the hill toward Ely and decided to take advantage of the elevation drop and sort of "blow the carbon out!"

I was near the bottom and me and old blue were "scootin through the dew" when I looked out of the corner of my eye at a gravel pit where you know who, old Smoky, had waited out a live one!

I pulled over and waited for him to pull up and come to the car.

He had a grin as wide as all outdoors when I rolled down the window. His words, "I didn't think it would go that fast either!"

The last of the Highway Patrolman stories finishes with a great amount of excitement.

We had been lion hunting up on the Nevada-Idaho line near Jarbridge, Nevada. My friend and helper, Lenny Jewell, had driven our Jeep station wagon with the dogs and snowmobile trailer up there and I had flown our Cessna 180-2242 Charlie up. I used it to look for lion tracks. We stayed at Murphy's Hot Springs on the Jarbridge River. It would be called a bed and breakfast today.

When we finished the hunt, I flew home and Lenny brought the Jeep again. I would get home a couple three hours before him and told him to come on out to the ranch in Clover Valley south of Wells. I would land at the airport in Wells and call someone to borrow some wheels or give me a ride the six miles out to the ranch.

I called Wanda Bordon and she and her husband, Charlie, brought their Oldsmobile car to the airport. I took them back to their home and borrowed their car to go to the ranch.

I got what I had to do done about dark and headed back to town. I figured I'd meet Lenny, return Wanda's car and ride back to the ranch with Lenny.

Of course Lenny didn't know what I was driving and I passed him in the dark about a mile south of Wells.

I screeched to a halt, turned around real fast and started after Lenny. I was going to just blink my lights to stop him.

The first blink with the dimmer switch and the lights went out! I'm hurtling along trying to keep it straight with where I thought the road should be and get it stopped when I looked in the mirror and, immediately, here came the dreaded blinking red light from somewhere!

I got it stopped without running off the road and jumped out to run back to the police car.

As I leaned over to talk to the policeman, I looked straight into business end of a shotgun barrel! A voice said, "What in the hell are you doing?"

I gave him the story and he replied, "I'm hid out waiting for a bank robber coming this way from Ely and you stop, turn around and race back the way you came and then turn out your lights! I was sure you were the one that had just robbed the Ely bank!"

Luckily he knew me – I got the lights to work and headed on toward home. Pretty weak in the knees, I might add!

Stan Potts and Lenny Jewell with a lion.

Chapter 10

Rodeoing Stories

When I was a kid and had contracted the dreaded "rodeo bug," trying to figure out how to practice the various events was a major problem.

When my folks would take me to a rodeo, I'd watch the cowboys and try to learn from them. (How the calf ropers rigged their horses, how the bulldoggers got from the horse to the steer and how the riding event cowboys equipment worked. Trying to figure out how to set a bareback rigging and a bronc saddle was, then, trial and error.

Practice stock for the riding events was a particularly major problem. I constructed a "bucking barrel" which gave me some practice, but real live animals that someone didn't mind being used as practice stock, were few and far between.

Jerry Twitchell and I practiced on his dad's milk cows. We bucked them out of the stanchions and down a steep hillside with a halter rope around their middle, which was pretty wild. That was relatively short-lived as his sisters ratted on us, plus Gerald wondered how come his milk production had tapered off quite "severiousley."

This was during the time when they were rounding up lots of wild horses (mustangs), around the West. Jack and Chuck Utter from Reno, Nevada, had a contract to deliver several hundred head to the stockyards in Mackay. They had a Piper Super Cub airplane plus some good horsepower and cowboys. They brought horses from as far away as the lower East Fork of the Salmon River – probably around fifty air miles.

They let us truck them from the stockyards over to the rodeo grounds and practice on them while they were waiting for the once-a-week train from Blackfoot. Once in a great while, there would be a good bucker and we would try to hold it back for an extra couple weeks practice. I remember one instance that turned out more than a little exciting for me.

Some rancher up on the east fork had been breaking a horse to ride. The story was that the horse had bucked him off out on the mountain, got away, and went with the mustang herd. The horse had a bridle and saddle on and they were not able to find him or at least to recapture him.

It takes a long time for cinches, latigos, leather, etc., to rot away but it finally happened and the horse lost the saddle and bridle. I would guess the horse ran around for several months before he lost the last of the tack. He had developed massive saddle sores during that period.

He was captured with the mustang gather and we figured he would be a good one to practice on.

Now, this horse had learned to not like people. We got him in the bucking chute and to say the least he was not a happy camper!

I had the good fortune, (misfortune?) to draw him as one of my practice horses that day. We had trouble getting the bareback riggin' on him as he would try to bite whenever anyone got within range. I got on him very carefully but, when I got my feet up by his shoulders, he turned his head and grabbed my left foot clear up on the instep in his teeth and would not let go!

Gerald Twitchell found a two by four board and tried to hit his head to make him let go but missed and hit me on the knee instead!

I said, "Turn him out, maybe he'll let go!" Probably not the best option but the only one I could come up with.

Sure enough, when the gate opened he turned loose of my foot and headed out into the arena, not bucking very hard but trying to bite my foot again. When the pickup man would get close the horse would take him!

I'm in a bit of a predicament, which could be termed an "understatement!" I know that however I get off, if he is able to, he will take me, with mouth wide open, and the results could be disastrous.

I finally made a flying dismount close to the arena fence and got up, over and away before he got me. It turned out better than it could have, believe me.

Jakes' Pickup Horse

One year before the Mackay rodeo, which is in late June, we had some good fortune on practice horses.

Jake Pope from Twin Falls had the stock contract for the rodeo and brought his horses a couple of weeks prior. We made him a deal to watch over his stock in return for using some of them to practice on.

Now, a lot of the horses we knew but one pretty sorrel that really bucked good – we didn't know. I said, "Man, I hope I draw that sorrel.

A guy could sure win the bareback riding on him!"

When Jake showed up and went to sorting his stock, guess where the sorrel went.? Into the pickup horses! I'd been bucking his saddle horse!

No, I didn't tell him!

When Joy and I got married we were not plagued with great quantities of extra money, more like in no money. We were getting ready to start haying and didn't have much equipment. We desperately needed a side delivery hay rake. We mowed the hay – let it cure in the sun and air for about a day and then it had to be raked into windrows to be picked up and baled a few days later.

The Mackay Rodeo would be starting in a day or two and we would start haying as soon as it was over. I borrowed $20.00 from my mom to enter the bareback riding. This was my best chance at "financing" the hay rake.

Well, I drew a good horse and did my job right. When the rodeo was over I had won the bareback riding and went over to Hershell Ivies Farm Equipment store and paid for a side delivery rake! One of the few times that this type of financing plan worked out!

These are a couple of funny rodeo stories that happened in Nevada.

The Winnemucca Rodeo was always a major event in our little world of rodeo. Held over the Labor Day weekend, it drew cowboys from five or six states and was always a good one.

This particular year I was bucked off in the bareback riding, into the fence on the far side of the arena. I crashed pretty hard and my head thunked a wooden post, kind of knocking me out. Lots of weird sensations, thoughts, feelings, etc, as you are passing in and out of consciousness.

This is the view from my perspective. The rodeo movie called "The Lusty Men" starring Robert Mitchum was fairly new and ended with a scene in a rodeo arena with the wind blowing tumbleweeds across an empty arena.

My view was of this movie scene, but evidently I was wandering around the arena with bucking horses, pick-up men, loose bulls etc, going by on both sides.

My view again – I went behind the chutes and sat down on my rigging bag. There was no one there. I thought, "They have left me and went home without me!" Then I'd get it back together and little more and see people and talk to them. I was slowly coming out of it.

We went out to the car and horse trailer and the trailer had a flat tire.

My view again – I can remember some of what happened.

Jack Anderson jacked it up to change its tire but the trailer was sort of shaky. He asked me to steady it while he changed the tire.

I remember standing there pushing on the side of the horse trailer and thinking, "Why am I standing here pushing on this trailer – people will think I am nuts."

You guessed it! I walked away and dropped the trailer!

Didn't hurt Jack to badly and he finally forgave me (several years later!).

One Fourth of July there were several rodeos going on in Nevada at the same time. Our little rodeo group of Jack Anderson, Gordon Wines and myself were going to hit them all! Just like the big boys. We had our wives with us, also.

We went to Carlin, then on to Fallon and back to Austin on the way home.

I started out first at Austin in the bareback riding. They had rounded up some mustangs for the bucking stock. My horse was a typical mustang – probably weighed eight or nine hundred pounds with me on him!

He jumped out of the chute high in the air – came down and stopped! I'd spur him, he'd jump again and stop. This was the way the whole ride went. Pretty ugly. Next, I roped a calf, poor catch and I wallowed him around in the alkali dust forever before I got him tied. Things weren't going very good.

I finished up with the team roping and the same thing, we used all the loops we were allotted and a couple trips around the arena. Very ugly once again.

I don't remember rodeoing so badly before or since. As soon as we finished we loaded up and left. We didn't want people laughing any more than they had already had at us Northern Nevada gunsels!

About a week later I got my checks for about $400.00. I had WON the all-around! Everyone else must have **REALLY** done bad!

Kay, Stani and Robyn Potts about the time of the Pine Nut Fiasco (see story on page 74).

Chapter 11

Get Rich Quick Schemes (Or, Where Did The Money Go!)

The Scotch Whiskey

Through the years I have tried several chancy" investments (other than buying ranches and outfitting businesses!)

You stumble along barely making ends meet and someone you know makes a big hit in the stock market or some other investment. You wish "Why didn't I do that?"

Here are a few of the tries I made.

Some friends of ours were investing in Scotch whiskey. No, not to drink but as in buying it in Scotland as it was being distilled and barreled and when it aged and was ready to market they sold it and made good money.

As usual, our investment didn't multiply. Timing again, I suppose. After a few years of paying storage, insurance, etc., and the whiskey not increasing in value at all, we decided we had two choices. They were: 1–go to Scotland and drink it! Or, 2 – walk away. We didn't think our livers would hold up under option 1!

Oil Wells

The second was investing in wildcat oil wells. You know, invest in several and one of them will come in and you will never work another day.

Now, not being wealthy, more like being church mouse poor, we had to figure out how to get money to buy in.

I had some life insurance policies I had been paying on for a long time, so we borrowed everything we could on those.

Put the money in several limited partnerships in wells so we would be rich – hah!

Usually it worked like this: they would get down 5,000 feet or so and we'd hear "Man, we know it's down there – another 2,000 feet and we'll have a gusher." We can smell the gas – we're nearly there." More money down the hole.

I'd already earned the nickname "Dry Hole" on the ranch water wells. Now I was enlarging on it with oil wells.

We finally gave up. We'd found another way to miss the "big hit"

But guess what, one well pumped about 2,500 gallons per minute of water! Out in an alkali desert in Utah where it couldn't be used for anything!

The Pine Nut Fiasco

Where we were ranching in Nevada was adjacent to many miles of pinon' pine forests.

The trees bear some sort of a nut crop at different elevations most every year so the birds and small mammals have something to survive on. An occasional year comes along with a super crop and people come from hundreds of miles away to camp out and harvest the nuts. A high percentage of these were doing it commercially with good money to be made on the rare "bumper crop" year.

The nuts had been a staple food for the Paiute Indians in the area and they still did some harvesting from the ranches and reservations.

Being perpetually poor around "Pottsville," we decided to participate in the harvest one good year with the idea of hopefully making a little much needed money plus having a good supply of pine nuts for ourselves.

Now, I had talked to my neighbors, Charlie Schoer and Bob Steele, two old-timers in Clover Valley, about the pine nut harvest. I had picked up what I perceived to be some valuable information to speed up the harvest process.

Bob was the first white child born in Clover Valley and I think Charlie was the second. They both liked to go to the town of Wells on Fridays for shopping, haircuts and a drink or two at the local bars. Bob was about ten years older than Charlie.

Charlie drove a pickup and he drove pretty slowly. Bob, on the other hand, had a big Cadillac and used it like a Caddy should be used. He would sometimes catch up to Charlie putting along in his pickup and pass him at the first opportunity. His words would be, "That kid is a lousy driver. He drives in the middle of the road!" Keep in mind that the road was a narrow, dirt, barely two-lane road in the good spots. Oh, Yes! Bob was in his late seventies and Charlie, "The Kid", was in his late sixties at

—74—

this point in time!

Back to the pine nuts. They told of people setting up a threshing machine so that the pine cones could be shelled to get the nuts separated from the cones. Hereby hangs my story.

Pine nut harvesting is a very slow, labor intensive process. I will give you a scenario of how it normally works.

The pinon' trees are from ten to twenty feet tall on the average. The cones are roughly the size of tennis balls with the largest the size of baseballs.

The cones have to be pulled off the limbs, sacked, taken home and laid out on a clean surface to dry. A few days in the sun causes the nuts to loosen in the cones so they can be shaken out and be placed in some sort of container.

To pull the cones from the trees, we used small poles about ten feet long with a nail driven in the end and bent to make a hook to pull the cones loose and let them fall to the ground.

We placed a big canvas beneath the trees to catch most of the cones so we could put them in gunny sacks to haul home to dry. Our three daughters, Kay, Robyn and Stani, were big enough to help. The pine nuts were worth somewhere around three to five dollars a pound and there was an unlimited amount of pounds in the forest. This may be the long awaited "Big Hit".

Unfortunately, we all knew how good the nuts were so a certain amount of time was spent by each of us getting the hulls off and sampling our crop to make sure we were into "Primo" nuts.

The first problem, (and ultimately the most major) hinged upon the fact that Pinon' pines are very resinous.

Now, three little girls with long hair crawling around on the ground picking up and sacking pine cones led to a major discovery upon our arrival back at the ranch with our first load. They were all stuck up and matted with pine tar! Hair glued together with the stuff and skin and clothes the same. It was a very tedious, slow and frustrating clean up job!

Anyway, we placed our prize collection of a pickup load of pine cones on a big canvas out in the sun to dry while I prepared my grain combine for the final phase of the process so we could take the nuts to town and market them

I adjusted the cylinders and concaves wide enough to allow the pine cones to go thru and, hopefully, separate the nuts from the cones like it was supposed to work.

After about three or for days of the cones drying in the sun, I moved the combine close to the pine cones for the initial test. Some minor adjustments and a never-ending stream of the chocolate brown nuts would flow from the grain tube into the hopper. Right?

I started up the combine, shoveled a few scoop shovels of pine cones into the header and moved around to the rear of the machine to be ready for the fine tuning of my adjustments.

About the time that the first cones come over the straw shakers and the first nuts dropped into the hopper my combine started lugging down and stopped. I opened up the inspection doors and you guessed it. Everything was coated and stuck together with pine gum!

It took me nearly a week to clean up my machine so I could go back to harvesting grain.

We hand-shelled the balance of our crop and filed "The Pine Nut Caper" under one more method of avoiding the "Big Hit."

Our luck wasn't as bad as two old guys from California. They had spent a couple months doing what we did – all by hand. They had a pickup and small trailer loaded with shelled pine nuts, probably several thousand dollars worth.

They were headed back to California and going through the little town of Deeth, Nevada, where the highway crossed the railroad tracks when their pickup stalled astraddle of the tracks.

The train come along and broadsided it, scattering their pine nuts and belongings in the cinders and dirt of the railroad fill for several hundred yards. It was impossible to retrieve or salvage any portion of their hard-earned crop. Now, that is real tough luck!

Chapter 12

The Frank Temoke Story

Author's Note – I thought the following story about my old friend and sometimes Team Roping partner, Frank Temoke, would be of interest. I would like to credit the author of the article excerpted here, Mary Branscomb, the artist, Don Farmer, and the Farm Times publication, which published this article in April of 1994, for their permission to use the story and pictures. Hope you enjoy. – Stan Potts

Heart of a Practical Joker Hides Behind Nonagerian's Poker Face
By Mary Branscomb

RUBY VALLEY, NV – It's apparent at first glance that Frank Temoke is both cowboy and Indian. His everyday clothes are a snap button shirt, pair of Levi's and broad-brimmed hat; but he wears eagle feathers and buckskin with equal ease and obvious pride as befits the chief of the Ruby Valley Shoshone tribe.

Frank started his cowboy career when he was 19 years old in northeastern Nevada's Ruby Valley where he was born in March of 1903. His first job was with Bill Gardner on the 7-H Ranch. Later, and for a total of 38 years, Temoke managed the North Ranch in Ruby Valley for different members of the Smith family.

While Frank ran cows, his wife Theresa (Knight) Temoke, who was born in the valley in 1912, was the ranch cook. She estimated they have been retired for 18 years.

Now, they live at Frank's father's place on Overland Creek. Of their seven children, five survived and they have "10 or 15 grandchildren" plus an uncounted number of great-grandchildren.

The couple also took one set of twins born to a daughter to rear as their own. Rocky Roa now lives in Elko, but he grew up with his grandfather at the foot of the Ruby Mountains learning a lot about life –

how to work, be a cowboy, love the mountains, understand his heritage and get along in the working world.

In the 1970s Roa became a successful rodeo cowboy, helped along by Frank and Theresa who put many miles on pickups and horse trailers as they hauled their grandson to rodeos.

Roa, who keeps his cattle on his grandparents' ranch, comes out every weekend. "Frank is like my dad," he explained. "I never saw him hit a horse or hotshot a cow, and I don't think I ever saw him prod a steer with a stick. And he never spanked – his disapproval was enough discipline for any of us." That included more than Temoke family members. Frank and Theresa raised a lot of children, both Indian and white, and they all "keep in touch."

"Don't do no good to hit," Frank observed. "Can't raise nobody if you're mad at 'em. They get scared of you."

He's lived in Ruby Valley all his life and claims his ancestors "lived here for as far back as anyone can remember."

He tells about his father, Ma-CHACH, who was kidnaped when he was a little boy and taken to New Mexico. About 10 years later, he returned on horseback.

The chief explains it was his direct ancestor, Chief Te-Moak (Joe Te-Moak), who in 19863 signed the Ruby Valley Treaty with the white man.

Frank has always participated in public events including an Elk High School band performance and city parades. In 1988 he was chosen grand marshal for the Silver State Stampede.

"Although he doesn't say much, Frank is always aware of what is going on in town and in the rest of the country," said Mike Gallagher, who owns an auto dealership in Elko. Since he was a young boy visiting the family ranch in Ruby, Gallagher has been the chief's friend.

"Sometimes when he comes in to get the oil changed in his pickup, he entertains tourists in the showroom," Gallagher said, smiling. "You know, Frank just looks like the Indian on the nickel, so he can get away saying almost anything and be believed."

"He spins wild yarns – with a poker face – about all the buffalo that used to be here until the white man came. The tourists believe him. They don't know there never were any buffalo in Nevada. He gets a big, private chuckle out of fooling people."

Frank also enjoys practical jokes. One story, still told after 30 years, is about several white hunters who camped on Indian land in Ruby

Frank Temoke in cowboy garb in a photo taken by Don Farmer.

Don Farmer's painting of Frank Temoke titled "His Feathers."

Valley and declined to leave when Frank informed them they were on reservation property.

He just rode out of camp and gathered up a few friends, giving the hunters time to take on a little too much "firewater." Then at dusk he led a mounted charge of whooping, wildly painted Shoshone over the brow of a hill and into the hunters' camp.

"It wasn't serious. He just likes to joke around," said his eldest son, J.R. Temoke.

Serious or not, the hunters moved – quickly.

Actually, the chief gets along well with his white neighbors. Every autumn he invites everyone in Elko to his home for an anniversary celebration of the signing of the Ruby Valley Treaty.

People pitch tents for the weekend or come for a day to watch a traditional ceremony conducted by the elders, or dance, play hand games and enjoy a barbecue.

One of the regulars who attends Frank's parties is Don Farmer, whom he helped get started in the right direction. Now a cowboy artist, Farmer spent months with the Temokes. Recently, he painted a portrait of Frank titled "His Feathers" and sells prints that show the famous chief in an eagle feather headdress.

"Frank seems like an ordinary cowboy when he wears his hat and glasses," Farmer said, "but I tell you when he takes them off he turns into somebody else. It's spooky how different he looks."

Farmer added: "If you want to have a conversation with him, you have to be patient. He's got a dry sense of humor – only there can be a long time between words."

Aside from his sense of humor, the chief has a sense of responsibility to his family and to his People, said daughter-in-law Lori Roa.

"He can remember how it was when the white man first came to the valley," she explained. "He is sad to see Shoshone traditions slipping away; so he tries to keep them alive by encouraging traditional gatherings and participation in Native American public events. He wants the people to be proud of who they are.

"He loves his white friends, too. In fact, Frank likes all people. He has something nice to say about almost everybody."

In his own way and following his own stars, Frank Temoke has lived successfully in two worlds for nearly a century.

Chapter 13

Poker Games

My father introduced me to some of the card games at an early age, primarily twenty-one, or blackjack as it is called, plus draw and stud poker.

Somehow I, like countless other misguided souls, decided I was a pretty good card player. Some times I did pretty well but as you will see, when I tried to play with the big boys, I got my feathers clipped.

We used to play on the school bus going and coming to ball games, track meets, etc. I usually could make four or five dollars playing penny ante on the course of a trip.

When I started rodeoing, there was usually a poker game to be found in someone's motel room and I made a few bucks at those games.

When I went to college at the University of Idaho, there was usually a never-ending poker game in our dormitories, the Campus Club and later the Idaho Club. Some of those guys I think were there for the poker games, with classes and study ranking a low second on the priority scale.

I remember one game that "clipped my wings" for the first time.

I was washing dishes at the student union for $.60 an hour. I was unloading ninety-pound gypsum sacks off of boxcars for $1.50 an hour. I had a football scholarship that paid $75.00 a month but you had to work at different jobs at the university to earn or justify it. I was a "hasher" (like a waiter) at the dormitory, which paid part of my room and board. We worked one week per month at meal times serving food and clearing the dining room after meals. This paid about half of my room and board and really helped.

You can see that extreme or even minimal wealth was not one of my problems. Accordingly, a few good hits in a game of chance would extend my "sheckel" supply.

Now, some of these card players were what I would rank as "very good," especially the mining engineers.

These guys spent there summers out in the real world learning the mining business first hand. A lot of them summered in Alaska and I don't know what they learned about mining, but they learned "Poker 101" very well.

The hand I remember to this day happened like this:

It was a five-card stud game and I was dealt a pair of queens the first two cards. I started "pushing" them about the third card and after four cards I had a pair of kings showing.

There didn't seem to be much power around the table after the last card, only a pair of threes that had shown on the last card. After the betting was over and the cards were shown, I looked at the third three from one of the mining engineers across the table to the tune of $57 of my hard-earned money!

The guy had read my bets like an open book!

That is a lot of dish washing at $.60 an hour, ninety-five hours worth! I had nightmares the rest of the night while trying to sleep; I replayed the hand a thousand times.

Good part of the news: I borrowed five dollars from my roommate the next night – got back in the game and got my money back! And, over the course of the school year I ended up $800.00 to the good. Between all my jobs, scholarship and poker winnings I finished one year of college with $200.00 from home! Lets see, three more years at $200.00 a year and I'd have a degree for $800.00.

Cobalt Poker Game

When we were mining at Cobalt, there was usually never-ending poker games going on. One shift would get off work, play, go back to work or home. The next shift would fill the vacant seats and so on.

My brother was working at the mine also and staying with us when we got our first paychecks. The checks were around $110.00 each after the "company store" bill and rent was taken out.

We wanted to get in the game so decided to cash one of the checks and keep the other one in case we didn't win!

They usually played straight draw or Texas poker – open on anything and draw all the cards you wanted.

Red Ankrum was running the game when I got in and he didn't explain that the game was now jacks or better.

I drew a four flush and bet it pretty heavy. A couple guys stayed in and I drew and missed my flush. I bet my hand heavy again and one guy called. When I turned my four flush over he jumped up and challenged me. Red realized I had thought we were playing straight poker, not jacks or better, and settled the guy down and took the heat off me. (As in possibly saving me from a bad "whipping"!)

Oh yeah, we lost the whole paycheck in our first endeavor. Easy come ($1.64) an hour as a miner. Easy go (push it into the pot) and lose!

The Wiener Pigs

About once a month while I was ranching in Nevada, some ranch would have a poker night and ranchers and hired men would show up for a night of drinks, food and poker till it was time to go to work in the morning.

One night the game was at my place, and along towards morning Tom Eldridge ran out of money. He had a bunch of wiener pigs and was betting them just like money.

Unfortunately, at the end of the evening, and in the morning, I was the owner of the pigs, which were at his place and I'd never seen them.

The next day I drove down to his ranch, knocked on his door and asked Tom's wife, Laurie, when she came to the door, if I could see the wiener pigs.

She said sure, "Do you want to buy some?" I said , "No, I just won them in the poker game!"

When Tom and Laurie got together that evening would probably not have been a good time to drop by for a visit!

The Sundown Poker Game – Literally!

When I moved to the Sun Valley area, it didn't take long to find where the poker games were.

Gambling as such was not legal but there was usually a "friendly" game going on in the Casino Bar in Ketchum. It took a $100 taw as an entry fee.

The dealer who ran the game also played and it didn't take too long till I ran up against the dealer in a five card stud game – beat him – and watched him cut the pot to get his loss back. I politely cashed in and didn't play there any more.

The other game ran a couple nights a week and had a system where you bought in with a $100.00 minimum. The dealer took $10.00 to cover meals, snacks, and drinks. Each buy-in after that was 10 percent also.

These guys played a lot of pretty wild games. Not straight poker –

usually high-low split with variations and wild cards – and although they were lots of fun, they were sometimes dangerous.

I had played off and on over a two or three year period and was ahead a little bit when the fateful night arrived.

The game started about 6:00 in the afternoon and the sun was still up. It was in a bunkhouse poker room and summertime – pretty warm so we had the doors open – one toward the setting sun, very apropos! Setting sun.

The game started with six people, just one short of a full table of seven players. The deal started to my left and was passed around the table to the left after each hand was played.

I bought my mandatory $100.00 worth of chips and immediately –as in first hand – lost it, knocking heads with the guy across the table.

I bought another $100.00 and "knocked heads" with the same guy and lost. Now, each time I was out "drawn out on" or "last carded" so I didn't feel like I was doing anything wrong. My turn would come but I felt like I needed more money so I bought in for $500.00 the third time.

I couldn't believe it – he got me on the last card again for the whole $500.00!

This can't go on forever, right?

I bought $500.00 more to prepare for battle once again.

It was like there were only the two of us playing. All the action and good cards ended up with just us two.

Now, once again, I had great cards, pushed them as in "charged the guy a lot of money" to draw two cards and got beat on the draw.

It was still one place from being my turn to deal. The deal had not got around to me yet. The sun was still shining and I was $1,200.00 poorer! Probably no more than thirty minutes had gone by.

I excused myself – thanked everyone for the lesson – and went home a legend from the Panting poker game, although not the kind of legend you want to be!

My paternal grandfather had been a gambler. Dad said when he was growing up it was chicken one day and feathers the rest of the month.

I decided I was not cut out to be a gambler and so went into a retirement mode!

Another Long Hunting Trip

In my first book, "The Pott's Factor Versus Murphy's Law," most people seemed to enjoy the hunting stories. Accordingly, I'm penning heretofore unpublished but campfire-related adventures here, hopefully for your enjoyment! There will be no chronological order to these – just as they come to mind.

Chapter 14

Wild and Mild – Hunts and Mountain Trips

Sadie the Mule

Before we bought the Chamberlain Basin hunting business, the seller showed the stock to me and gave me a rundown on each animal.

Most of them had sort of ordinary names like Jack, Jenny, Henry and Donna. We finally got to a big black molly mule called "Sadie."

Something about the name conjured up visions of future problems. When I watched the owner walk the front feet of the mule into an open lariat loop just to put the halter on, I was pretty sure I was right!

The old Hotzel Cabin in the Chamberlain Basin where Sadie the Mule was shod. The cabin burnt down in the forest fires of 2000.

We went ahead and bought the outfit and I used the mule all I could to try and mellow her out. She was big, stout and tough but you could tell she had got the bulge on lots of packers before me.

When it came time for shoeing, I decided I'd try to shoe her standing up with no foot ropes.

Bad mistake!

I got the left front on with only minimal problems. Then I started the left rear and after fifteen or twenty minutes was getting kicked and beaten till I gave up.

I put the mule on the ground and even with her feet tied up, she was torturing me worse than you can imagine.

Ultimately, I had a pole about five inches through and twenty feet long over her rib cage and tied solid to her feet. My friend, Dick Hall, sat on the end of the pole and I finally got the rest of the shoes nailed on. I was so stiff and sore I could hardly walk for a week.

A guy came by with a big black gelding named "Checkers" that wanted to trade his gelding. Guess where Sadie went?

The New Jersey Hunters
Some of our first hunters at Chamberlain Basin.

When we bought the outfitting business in Chamberlain Basin here in Idaho we needed to locate some paying customers to try and pay for the business and cover the bills. We ran a small ad in *Outdoor Life* magazine and sat back to wait for the customers to flock to our new business.

The business didn't have a name so we decided to capitalize on the notoriety of the area in the hunting world and named it "Chamberlain Basin Outfitters." Pretty catchy, eh?

Anyway, I received a call from a gentleman in New Jersey (I won't be using names in this chapter). After you read it you will probably realize why. He had a flower shop and was the point man or contact person for a group that wanted to come West on a hunting trip.

I was able to book their group of six on a guided hunt for the seasons opening in mid-September.

When they arrived and we sort of got to know them, we found out that they were all of Italian-Sicilian descent and important members of a notorious group that operated somewhat on the shady side of the law. There is a name for them known around the world that I'm sure you are familiar with but I hesitate to put it in print even after the forty years since this occurred.

These gentleman were not a bit bashful about explaining their line of work. In fact, it appeared to be a badge of honor and success with them.

They each had small businesses, like cigar stores, print shops and flower shops that they admitted were only to present a legitimate front for some activities that were occasionally on the opposite side of accepted and legitimate customs.

Three of them were brothers. They were evidently quite well known in their circle and were frequent name droppers of some of their friends in the political world and the entertainment industry.

They told us what they claimed to be the intimate details of Marilyn Monroe's death. This was several years prior to any details coming out of the media. Their version turned out to be very close to what was published and circulated.

They brought their own attorney along. I was not sure of all the reasons but he was a good hunter and, like all the members of the group, an excellent shot.

We were visiting one day and he told me an interesting story.

The New Jersey hunters.

He was hunting polar bears in the Arctic from a sailing ship and had the misfortune of dropping his expensive rifle overboard.

He laughed as he explained, "When I got home, three insurance companies had each paid for it!"

I sent their group to one of our spike camps at Hot Springs Meadows with two guides, Floyd Posing and Gary Bean, and Gary's wife, Bonnie, as a cook for their one-week hunt. I had three California hunters, Steve Erm and his sons-in-law, Bill, and Jim, who would hunt with me around the Hotzel Ranch that we had leased from the Idaho Department of Fish and Game as a base for our operations.

Along in the middle of the first night the entire New Jersey group of hunters, plus our help, descended back at the ranch with three elk.

They didn't like the area I had sent them to because they had only killed three elk the first day and hadn't seen any more! Also, they didn't like to live in tents and the cook was in tears because they didn't like her cooking.

Subtle negotiation time had arrived!

I told them they could hunt from the ranch with a cabin and beds and I would send the California hunters back to Hot Springs with a guide and

Bill Butts, Steve Erm and Jim from Sacramento in front of the meat house at the Hotzel Ranch.

the cook. I also explained that they had left the area with the most elk.

They seemed happy. (I think because of the cabin and beds!)

I sent the most junior guide that I had employed with the three brothers to the East of the Hotzel Ranch to hunt Little Lodgepole Creek. He rode them over to the only open sagebrush knob in the area and about noon tooted on his elk bugle. (Keep in mind that this kid had probably never seen a live elk in the wilds!)

He received and answer and immediately a giant bull came running up this open hill to the horses and hunters – probably not the smartest thing the elk had ever done.

That evening their attorney said, "That bull committed suicide. No sensible elk is safe around three (enter a fitting name) brothers with guns in their hands!"

Joy started cooking for the transplant group and she mutinied {as in quit} after the first day of their return. She politely, well maybe not politely, informed them. "Gentleman, the kitchen is yours."

However, they didn't even like each other's cooking and fought and argued constantly about how to season the spaghetti, how long to boil it, how long to cook the steaks, etc.

We had a little log meat house to keep the bears out of the meat. Joy was out cutting some steaks from a hind quarter when the quarter fell down on her. Some of the group were standing there watching and remarked, "Boy, you're pretty strong for a little woman as she crawled out from under it."

However, no one offered to help her!

Come In Albuquerque!

The following anecdotes are a collection of more hunting, packing and mountain living stories gathered over the years.

One year about 1968, we were hunting sheep out of the Taylor Ranch on Lower Big Creek in what was then called The Idaho Primitive Area.

It is a approximately fifty miles by trail to get into that country, with a landing strip at the Taylor Ranch plus another one three miles down Big Creek at Soldier Bar. (Soldier Bar was named in honor of the last soldier killed in an Indian war in the United States, Private Harry Eagan, who had died there from a gunshot wound about ninety years before.) A memorial plaque had been shipped by the government by train, wagon and pack mule to Cougar Dave Lewis. Cougar Dave had mustered out of the army at the end of the Civil War and then went to work for the army as a civilian packer during the Sheepeater Indian War of 1879.

He was there when Private Eagan died and after the Indian Campaign he stayed in that country and eventually homesteaded what is now the Taylor Ranch. He built the rockwork monument for and installed the plaque in later years, after the airstrip was constructed. He was probably the only one around who knew the location of the grave or any of the details of Private Eagans' death.

My two guides, Dick Hall and Fay Detweiler, plus my wife Joy and I, had been in the mountains for a couple of weeks scouting for sheep, learning the country and building a camp to hunt out of.

Our hunters, (Don Ammon, Roy Woodward and Fred LaBean) from Flint, Michigan, had arrived and we were ready to hunt sheep.

We had little walkie-talkie radios which usually didn't work very good or very far. You were usually trying to contact someone instead of talking to them.

Also, Fay had a small radio for news of the outside world. It worked early in the morning, usually.

It was the custom of the guides to meet in the cook tent several hours before daylight to go over the day's plans before we wrangled the stock

From left are Don Amon, Fay Detweiler, Roy Woodward, Fred LaBean and Stan Potts.

and before the hunters come in for breakfast. This was also the time of the best radio reception for Fay's radio. Usually, Albuquerque was the station that came in the best.

This particular morning Fay couldn't pick up the station. I looked across the table and he had the radio held up to the side of his head saying "come in Albuquerque, come in Albuquerque!"

We all had a good laugh and told him he had been in the mountain too long!

Guide Dick Hall and his ram, which was taken after the hunters had left.

Guide Fay Detweiler. "Come in Albuquerque".

Jingles

We had a black mustang mare in the outfit that I had traded for down in Nevada. Her name was "Star" and she was a sweetheart. She had, probably, the best night vision I have ever been around. She become our "bell mare," to keep the mules together while they were turned loose to graze. We were raising mules at the time and we had two Jacks, "Jocko" and "Sambo" that we just ran loose with the mares.

One fall we had gone back to the telephone camp to hunt. We turned the stock loose on the mountain in the evening and the next morning I would find them in the dark by the sound of the bell. I heard the bell up north of camp and started up the hill with a little bread sack of grain and a halter for Star. I would catch her and the rest would follow the sound of the bell back to camp.

As I worked my way up the mountain – the sound was probably three-quarters of a mile out and 1,000 feet up – I would occasionally hear the bell clanging like it was Star running full bore. I actually wondered what was chasing her, except as I got closer the clanging sounded like the bell came from the same location even though the noise indicated Star was still running.

Star, the "Bell Mare," at Telephone Creek Camp about the time of Jingle's birth.

I finally got where my flashlight would shine on the stock and then walked up to catch Star. There, under her neck, was a little black baby mule creature with its nose on Star's bell, making it ding like she was running full blast!

We had no idea Star was with foal but evidently the long trip back there had brought the birth on a little prematurely. The little mule got up, nursed and decided he loved the sound of that bell and learned how to clang it with his nose when his mother wasn't moving.

"Jingles" became his name and he was a character. He had over 300 miles on his little feet before he was a month old. He was so smart that he figured out if he could work his way up to the front end of the string and stop in the trail that he would get to rest when he wanted to.

I don't know if he is still going now but I saw him a few short years ago, gray-headed but still going strong and nearly thirty years old.

Ken Johnson and the Rocket Mule!

One fall we were headed back from the Taylor Ranch to our Telephone Creek camp for the opening of elk season. Long-time friend and client Ken Johnson was along on the trip and we had a couple of pack strings following the hunters along the "Dead Horse Trail."

I was leading the string directly behind the hunters with Ken in the back of that group. Ken didn't care for horses all that much but called them a necessary evil to get to the hunting country.

One of the rear mules in my string had a five gallon propane tank barrel hitched on one side. Somehow another mule got a lead rope up on top of this pack and it opened the valve on the tank!

Now you have to realize and visualize the ensuing commotion! The gas vapor is a white-colored gas under pressure and when escaping from an open valve is a very noisy SWISSSSSSHHHHH – probably in the volume range of a high-pitched wide-open jet engine!

My usually gentle string of semi-domesticated quadripeds became somewhat agitated – as in, they are coming after me like the last 100 yards at Santa Anita! I hollered at the hunters up ahead to clear the trail

The telephone cabin.

– speed up, save their own lives first!

Some of the hunters and Joy got off the trail but Ken continued straight ahead! When I would get a glimpse of him, he was jockeyed up like Eddie Arcaro and outrunning the charging string!

After several hundred yards, with mules breaking loose and leaving the trail, the rest tangled up where I could get the valve shut off and get regrouped. Another exciting day "movin' west!"

Stan Potts and Ken Johnson with one of the three biggest mountain lions killed in the United States in 1974. The lion is Number Two in the 1985 Nevada Record Book.

Constipation Ridge

The name for this chunk of real estate was coined by some of our hunters from Texas – Rocky Ford, Herb Harris, Preston Ross and Richard Henderson.

When we were unable to find elk close enough to hunt from a main camp, we would take a grill, sleeping bags, foam pads and a sheet of plastic and lay out on the mountain to try and get some elk. One of these "Siwash" camps was not so fondly named Constipation Ridge!

The group was from Midland Texas and hunted with us for several years. Rocky Ford owned a large trucking firm based out of Midland. He was probably the guy that was the spitting image of peoples idea of a Texan. About six-feet four-inches, 260 pounds and a voice that – when he whispered – would bend aspen trees fifty yards away!

Rocky had a ranch also and was a good horseman. I remember the very first time they hunted with us. I was somewhat short of riding stock and when they got off the airplane, I wondered, "what horse am I going to put the big guy on?"

I still hadn't figured it out when I was saddling up in the morning.

As usual, the hunters were standing around watching the proceedings and usually somewhat in the way. I had a buckskin three-year-old colt named "Hungry" that we were breaking. I'd thrown a saddle on him and hitched him to the rail and was saddling more stock trying to get a feel for a horse for Rocky.

About then Rocky walked over to Hungry and in this order said, "Which one do you want me to ride? How about this one?"

He grabbed the latigo and nearly lifted Hungry off the ground as he cinched him. He turned him around while I was still trying to come up with an answer and stepped on!

Hungry sort of squatted-braced himself – and then walked off as pretty as you please!

I had noticed that when Rocky got on, he had bent over and reached down and put the right stirrup over his boot. I just thought the stirrup was turned wrong but there is more to this story.

I told Rocky, "Ya, that one will be fine." Hungry packed him the whole hunt with no problems! Hungry couldn't have weighed over 900 pounds. I don't know to this day how he did it except he was one of those little horses with a heart as big as a bowling ball!

From left are Rocky Ford and Preston Ross.

I had guided Rocky for several days and while walking I would hear a "squish-squish" behind me. It sounded like someone walking with a rubber boot full of water.

Then, I found out Rocky had stepped on a land mine in Germany and his right leg was gone at the knee! He had a "wooden leg." That is why he couldn't put his foot in the off side stirrup!

Another part of the story: We were always throwing rocks at the grouse trying to get one to add to the dinner.

Preston Ross was the vice president of Rocky Ford Van Lines and was the comedy part of the group. He said he was pretty good with a sling shot-bean flipper type weapon. We found a perfect, forked willow, I took some inner tube off of my saddle horn and we were all ready except for a piece of leather for the bucket or part that holds the stone when you pull it back to launch it at the unexpecting grouse.

Preston said he knew where there was some leather and would get it that night. Sure enough, in the morning he showed up with a nice piece of leather about four inches square for our bean flipper.

When Rocky woke up, I heard a big scream from his tent. Preston had cut a piece of leather out of his prosthesis!

Preston must have been a pretty good employee to get away with cutting a piece of leather out of his bosses "wooden leg!"

Oh, and by the way – Preston wasn't lying about his prowess with the "bean-flipper." We had several tasty meals of blue grouse from the "community weapon." But Preston was the marksman!

Herb Harris was an attorney in Midland and a physical fitness nut; he stayed in very good shape. Jess Taylor was guiding for me, and I teamed he and Herb Harris one day. That night, during the "cocktail hour," Herb said, "The first two hours I stayed right with him step for step – after that it was a fight for survival!" Jess was about 70 years old then and had only one lung!

These guys brought the hottest jalepeno peppers I have ever been around. Herb would ride his Harley Davidson bike a few hundred miles down into Mexico and bring them back from a little cannery down there. Their hors de'oeuvres consisted of big slices of white onion covered with jalapeno peppers, washed down with Scotch whiskey!

Richard was the Beechcraft airplane dealer in Midland and although the Taylor ranch strip is not really a Beechcraft Bonanza strip, he would bring a new Bonanza in each year. The attorney, Herb Harris, had been a fighter pilot during World War II but other than being the co-pilot

Stan Potts landing at Taylor Ranch.

occasionally on their trips, hadn't flown much as pilot in command for many years.

One year Richard shot a mule deer buck up by Rush Point lookout. As he was hurrying down the hill to the deer, Richard fell and broke his leg.

The guide, Jim Martini, got a horse and was able to get Richard back to the Rush Point camp where we were based. He then rode to the Taylor Ranch where Joy radioed out for the helicopter.

I had showed up at the ranch during these proceedings and waited for the chopper to show him where to go. When the chopper arrived, we went up to Rush Point where the pilot hovered the chopper on a sidehill so we could get Richard loaded. Then Herb Harris rode back down to the ranch with us, as he had to be the pilot to fly the Bonanza out.

I'll never forget the look on Herb's face as Richard was telling him the procedures for short field take off. Herb was laying in the stretcher in the chopper and Herb was almost hanging on the side to get the last advice as the chopper lifted into the air to go to Boise. The look could probably be described as "apprehensive to the max!"

I had Rocky and Preston in my Cessna 180 and Herb had some of the gear in the Bonanza. I told him I would take off first and he could follow me. After we got enough altitude, he could throttle back and follow me as the weather was somewhat marginal and we would probably have some detours.

I looked back and Herb and the Bonanza looked like a Lear Jet as it climbed out behind me. He definitely did it all right.

How Do They Know?

Through the many years and many trips along the mountain trails, I've seen some monstrous pack train lash ups as well as some instances of animals behavior that was near perfection for which I still have trouble explaining.

I want to relate an instance that could have been certain death to a packstring if they had not done things right.

The wilderness where we outfit has been burnt over by massive forest fires in several places since the inception of the Forest Service "Let Burn Policy." (See the picture collage on pages 84-89 in my book *"The Potts Factor versus Murphy's Law"* for an idea of the devastation.) Some of the areas in those pictures have burnt three and four times since the 1988 fire.

Moving along the trail and cleaning still-burning logs.

One of these fires was about 1994 and had the forest closed to access for a couple of weeks in early August. This was right when we had to be packing supplies and camps in if we were going to be able to operate during the fall hunting season.

The Forest Services finally opened the area to access but there were still small isolated areas burning throughout the area.

Three of us, Tom McCollum, Jim Colyer and I, headed in with a packstring load of camp gear. When we get to the North Fork of Stoddard Creek, we could see smoke and flames up ahead of us where the trail went up the canyon. Tom and Jim walked ahead, rolling smoking burning logs out of the trail. They would go a few hundred yards to make sure it was passable, then holler that it was clear and I would bring the packstring and their riding horses; then, I'd wait for them to scout and clear another stretch of trail.

The trail is on a steep slope a hundred yards or so above Stoddard Creek. We had made it part way through the worst of the smoke and fire and I waited for them to move ahead and work another stretch of trail. The ground cover was mostly covered with ashes and smoking limbs but

My grandfather, Herb Gray, and a mule team. Maybe that's why I like the long-eared devils!

some of the redstem and willows had not burned. However the ground and air was very hot.

They called me ahead and I was moving just a few feet above a patch of redstem and brush that had not burned when it erupted in flames from spontaneous combustion! The flames were only six to eight feet from my string and were burning over one hundred yards down the steep slope to the creek.

How the pack stock were able to maintain calm and move along the trail in single file, I will never know. We probably had to go fifty to seventy five yards that way before we got ahead of the flames.

If any one of them had panicked and jerked the string off the trail, they would all have been fried as they rolled through the flames! Sometimes you just want to give those long-ears a kiss! This was one of those times except there wasn't time nor a place to do it. A single "thanks guys" was the best I could do, but I guarantee you it was with all sincerity!

PHOTO SECTION

My first year as an outfitter in 1958 with a couple of my clients' bucks. I am 24 years old.

— NEVADA HUNTS —

DEER BY DRAWING ONLY
— 4-DAY HUNT - $150 —

DESERT BIGHORN BY DRAWING ONLY
— TWO-WEEK HUNT - $1500 —

Write Nevada Fish and Game Commission,
P.O. Box 10678, Reno, Nev. for applications.

Roy Woodward   Fred LaBean   Don Amon
Onaway, Mich.   Flint, Mich.   Flint, Mich.

Shown with 3 of 9 rams taken in 1968

— ☆ — ★ — ☆ — ★ — ☆ —

Chamberlain Basin Outfitters

Fly-in Only

LICENSED — BONDED — INSURED
Member Idaho Outfitters Association,
Nevada Guides and Packers Association

After 10 years outfitting Nevada & Idaho - Age 34

During Hunting Season
Phone Boise 208-344-0497 via 2-way radio

PLAN A HUNT WHERE YOU SELDOM SEE ANOTHER HUNTER

For Elk, Deer, Bear, Sheep, Goat or Mountain Lion in Idaho's Primitive Area

Hunts Start From Hotzel Ranch in Unit 20-A At The Chamberlain Basin Airstrip or Taylor Ranch in Unit 26 — A Two-Deer Area

Hunting seasons generally start first Saturday in September for Mountain Sheep and Mountain Goat. Goat by drawing only. Sheep hunts from Taylor Ranch only.

—14-DAY HUNT - $1000 PER PERSON—

In 1968 we took 9 rams for 100% success

Elk, Deer and Bear Seasons Generally Open 3rd Saturday in September to Mid-December

— 10-DAY HUNT FOR ELK AND DEER —
$400 Per Person

— TROPHY BULL AND BUCK HUNT —
$750, With Individual Guide

21-Day special combination hunt. Sheep, Elk, Deer and Bear, $1500.

In 1968 49 Elk were killed for 75% success

For any of these hunts everything is furnished but license, tags, guns, sleeping bags and transportation to ranches.

License $100, Elk Tag $3.00, Deer Tag $2.00, Sheep Tag $10.00, Goat Tag $10.00.

All Hunts Subject to 3% Sales Tax

— 25% Deposit Required On All Hunts —

Round-trip flying costs average $60 from Challis and McCall. $75 to $100 from Boise, airline connections available at Boise, Idaho.

IDAHO OR NEVADA MOUNTAIN LION HUNTS

During Fall, Winter and Early Spring When the Lions are in full fur

— LION GUARANTEED - $500 —

STEELHEAD FISHING - APRIL AND MAY
CHINOOK SALMON - JUNE AND JULY
TROUT - JUNE TO NOVEMBER

We have several lakes and streams within a few minutes walk to ½-days pack from the ranches.

Let us arrange a pack trip or trail ride for photography, fishing or sight seeing.

— For a relaxing trip bring the family —

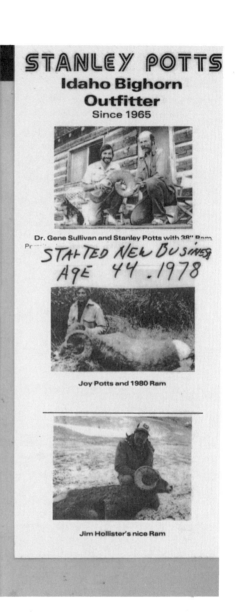

STANLEY POTTS
Idaho Bighorn Outfitter
Since 1965

Dr. Charles Guess and beautiful trophy Ram

1981 Ram taken by Stanley Potts
Boone and Crockett score 184 4/8

Earnie Sanders & 1983 Ram

Write or phone: Stanley Potts, Box 1122, Hailey, Idaho 3333. Phone: (208) 788-4584.

A FEW FACTS ABOUT ELK HUNTING & TAG & LICENSE SALES

Deer & Elk tags will be on first come, first served basis for 1978 and sold only until approximately Oct. 1st. Send license and tag money to the Idaho Fish & Game Dept., 600 South Walnut Street, Box 25, Boise, Idaho 83707 as soon as possible to assure your getting a license and tags.

Hunters will furnish license, tags, guns, rifle scabbards, sleeping bags, air mattress, meat sacks, and fishing gear. Stream fishing is available through late October.

We feel that more of our elk hunters would be successful if a few facts were known — especially among novice hunters. Sometimes you will only get one chance at elk during you hunt.

While Hunting—
1. Wear light wool pants and wool jacket or shirt on top. The nylon jackets are too noisy.
2. Keep noises to a minimum: voices, rattling bullets, loading rifles, frozen pant cuffs, etc., can easily ruin your hunt.
3. If your guide leaves you on a stand — stay there until the time you're supposed to leave.
4. If you are hunting with the guide — follow in his EXACT footsteps, about six feet behind. The guide will try to alleviate unnecessary noise.
   The above procedure will aid your guide in obtaining maximum results for a successful hunt.
5. Try to get legs and lungs in shape to walk a few miles. Sometimes this is necessary.
6. If you follow these rules your guide will have a much better chance at getting you a good shot at an elk.

Peter Merlin — Chicago, Illinois

LICENSED BONDED INSURED
Member Idaho Outfitters and Guides Association

- CALL OR WRITE -
Con Hourihan
Clover Valley
Wells, Nevada 89835
Phone: (702) 752-3718
During hunting season
Phone: Challis, Idaho 208-879-2372 via 2 way radio

Stanley Potts Outfitters
Wilderness Hunting & Fishing Trips
Since 1965 In Idaho

Jack Basolo at Stoddard Lake with Cutthroat Trout

First 5 Elk and Deer Hunts are 9 Days. Last 2 are 7 Days.

ELK & DEER
Trip #1 - Pack train elk & deer hunts start Sept. 15-Sept. 25, Oct. 5, Oct. 15, Oct. 25, Nov. 4, & Nov. 12, private elk & deer hunt for 1 to 6 persons. Use of entire hunting area including all spike camps, guides, equipment, etc., must be reserved in advance of any bookings for a particular hunt period. Price $18,000.

Trip #2 - Individually guided hunt for elk & deer. Price $4,000 per person.

Trip #3 - Hunt for elk & deer. Two hunters per guide. Price $3,000 per person.
(NOTE: No extra charge to hunt bear also.)

SHEEP
Trip #4 - (Early Sept. thru late Oct.) 10 day pack-train Rocky Mountain and California Bighorn Sheep Hunts. Permits by drawing—make arrangements by March 1. Includes one guide plus wrangler/spotter. Price $6,180 per person.

Trip #5 - 10 day backpack Bighorn Sheep hunts. Individual guide. Price $4,635 per person. (We have taken 38 rams since 1965.)

FISHING
Trip #6 - (July and August) 7 day pack train high mountain lake fishing & photography trips. 3 person min./10 person max. Price $875 per person.

NOTE: Non-hunting guests $130 per day on all hunting trips.

5% sales tax added to all trips.

DEPOSIT POLICY: 25% at time of booking, 25% by April 1. Balance 30 days prior to trip.

SHEEP HUNT DEPOSITS: 50% at time of booking.

NO REFUNDS ON DEPOSIT MONEY!

HUNTING SEASON EMERGENCY PHONE NUMBER:
208-756-4713

RECOMMENDED GEAR LIST FOR NINE DAY HUNT:
Big Game Rifle (sighted in for 200 yds) you are familiar with and can handle, plus 40 rounds of cartridges. Use proven loads and bullets that will hold together when they hit.

Enough meat sacks to hold 4 quarters of elk meat plus two for deer.

Binoculars.

Waterproof match container.

Good pocket knife. (Belt knife in good scabbard is okay. I prefer the folding blade models.)

Fanny pack or small day pack. (For lunches, snacks, flashlight, camera etc.)

Small flashlight. (Pocket model with extra batteries and bulb.)

Small camera and extra film. Extra eyeglasses if you wear them and sunglasses if you need them for snow or glare.

Small overnight bag with towel, washcloth, soap, chapstick, toothbrush and any prescriptions.

Good sleeping bag. If you want to bring air mattresses, okay.

One pair leather gloves and one pair warm gloves or mittens.

Good set of rain gear or poncho. Preferably green or camouflage color. (The plastics tear.)

Well broken-in leather hunting boots with Vibram soles.

Two pairs wool or felt insoles. Four changes light wool socks. Four changes nylon or silk socks.

Hunting hat or cap with visor and earmuffs. Wool pullover cap. Light long johns.

AFTER APPROXIMATELY OCTOBER 15 ADD THE FOLLOWING GEAR:
Heavy wool coat, wool pants and wool socks. Heavy long johns. Insulated pacs with Vibram or comparable soles.

Please feel free to adjust this list up or down to your own preference but you should be able to get everything but your rifle into one or two canvas duffle bags with a total weight of approximately 60#.

We will furnish foam pads for sleeping and rifle scabbards if you need them.

If you have any dietary or food preferences beyond normal camp fare, please let us know.

STANLEY POTTS OUTFITTERS

1997

Idaho License 296 · Bonded · Insured

Wilderness Trophy Deer, Elk, Sheep Hunting and Fishing Trips Since 1964 in

IDAHO

1996 Idaho Sheep Lottery Winner - Dr. Kevin Moore, San Diego, CA
Our 56th Ram!

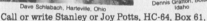

Dave Schlabach, Harteville, Ohio | Guide Jeff Waite & Dennis Gratton, Boise, Idaho

Call or write Stanley or Joy Potts, HC-64, Box 61, Shoup, Idaho 83469

Phone · 208-394-2135 · Fax

Hunting Season Emergency Number 208-756-4713

STANLEY POTTS OUTFITTERS

1997

Will BE our 40th YEAR. Cant wait to see what will happen next! im 62.

ALLIANCE TITLE & ESCROW CORP.

Chris Tillitson, Minneapolis, MN with "The Growler Bull" | John Walsh, Boca Raton, Florida 1996 Non-Typical Mule Deer

Call or write Stanley or Joy Potts, HC-64, Box 61, Shoup, Idaho 83469

Phone · 208-394-2135 · Fax

Hunting Season Emergency Number 208-756-4713

Elk - Deer Hunting

The season just ended turned out pretty well in spite of several hunts conducted in inclement weather conditions (i.e., fog, lengthy storms, etc.) The bulls did bugle pretty good also.

Our guided hunters ended up with 5 bulls for 10 hunters and the unguided hunters with 3 bulls for 8. Several clients passed on smaller bulls waiting for the big one. We also took a couple nice bears and 4 bucks including a big 6 by 7 and a 5 by 5. We had a good winter in 95/96 and above average moisture during the summer which reflected itself in the horn growth. The antler size was considerably better than in the past few seasons. (Hope this trend continues!)

Dr. John Pennings, Coeur d'Alene, Idaho
His first bull! 1996

We had a fun experience on the Nov. 4 hunt when Channel 7 television from Boise filmed a few days of the hunt for Idaho Public Television, The Idaho Dept. of Commerce and the Idaho Outfitters Association. It will also air on the Outdoor Channel so if you get a chance to watch it you will see a typical old time elk hunt in wilderness conditions. Mike Keating, the hunter that took the only bull we were able to get on while the film crew was there informed me that this was his sixth bull on eight trips. I told him not to let that get out or everybody would be expecting that kind of success!

It doesn't appear that there will be any major changes in the elk and deer seasons or regulations for the 1997 season but, major changes are possible and probable for the seasons beyond 1997.

Tags will go on sale again on Dec. 16 - first come basis for nonresidents so if you are planning a hunt for 1997 - get your group organized early. Several groups waited to long last year and the tags were all sold out.

I had a good year on my hunting also, getting a small bull moose and a small bull elk, so we have our winters meat!

Getting to know us ...

For those of you that are not familiar with us, we live at Colson Creek which is about 58 miles down the Salmon River, West of Salmon, Idaho. Our elk, deer and some sheep areas start 3 miles further down the river. We are about 3 hours driving time from Missoula and Butte, Montana and approximately four 4 hours from Idaho Falls, Idaho. Guests flying into one of these towns usually rent a car and drive to Colson Creek. They plan their arrival for the evening prior to departure with the pack string. Rooms and meals are available at the Ramshead Motel 3 miles up river from Colson Creek. We will gladly make reservations for you if you so desire. We have breakfast at our camp at Colson at 6:00 A.M. on the morning of the trips departure.

There are meat processing plants and taxidermists in Salmon. We do not charge for caping of trophies and will deliver your meat and trophies for processing as per your instructions. Processing costs and airfreight to your closest commercial airport will be your responsibility. Call some of our references, give us the dates you would like to come and we will try to accommodate you. Remember, we are a small family operation, cater to small groups and handle only a very small number of clients each year.

Elk and Deer tags are on a first come basis and some sell out in midwinter. If you plan on hunting with us we will get them for you upon receipt of the proper fees and vital statistics.

Sincerely,
Stan & Joy Potts

Non-Resident License/Tag Costs	
License	$101.50
Elk	326.50
Deer	226.50
Bear	226.50
lion	226.50
Sheep is by drawing .... DEADLINE IS 4/30!	906.50
Fishing - Season	51.50
- Daily $7.50 - $3.00 each additional day.	

Information For License

Name _____
Home Address _____
City _____ State _____ Zip Code _____
Phone _____ Social Security No. _____
Sex _____ Height _____ Weight _____ Birthdate _____

ELK, DEER, SHEEP & FISHING TRIP PRICES

First 5 Elk and Deer Hunts are 9 Days. Last 2 are 7 Days.

Trip #1 - Pack train elk and deer hunts start Sept. 15 - Sept. 25, Oct. 5, Oct 15, Oct. 25, Nov. 4 and Nov. 12, private elk and deer hunt for 1 to 6 persons. Use of entire hunting area including all spike camps, 3 guides, cook equipment, etc. must be reserved in advance of any bookings for a particular hunt period. Price $18,800.

Trip #2 - Individually guided hunt for elk and deer. Price $4,400 per person.

Trip #3 - Hunt for elk and deer. Two hunters per guide. Price $3,300 per person (NOTE: no extra charge to hunt bear also.)

Trip #4 - Unguided Hunts - Four person minimum. Spike camp elk and deer hunts. We furnish set up tent camp with stoves, cooking and camp gear, cots & foam pads, check to pack in meat about every 3rd day, pack in and out, horses to ride in and out only, no horses in camp to hunt on. Hunters furnish own food. Price $1,650 per person. Plus $300 per elk, $100 per deer and $100 per bear - meat packing charge.

Trip #5 - Deluxe Unguided Hunt - Includes food and cook in addition to conditions of Trip #4. Price $2,250 per person.

Trip #6 - (Early Sept. through late Oct.) 10 day pack-train or 4WD Rocky Mountain and California Bighorn Sheep Hunts. Permits by drawing - make arrangements by March 1. Includes one guide plus wrangler/spotter. Terrain and area will dictate horses, vehicles or both. Price $6,780 per person.

Trip #7 - 10 day backpack Bighorn Sheep hunts. Individual guide. Price $5,080 per person.

NOTE: Non-hunting guests $145 per day on all hunting trips.

5% SALES TAX ADDED TO ALL TRIPS.

DEPOSIT POLICY: 25% to 50% at time of booking, at least 50% by April 1. Balance 30 days prior to trip. No refunds on deposit money.

If you want to buy Trip Cancellation Inusrance call 1-800-452-2567 or 208-935-0726

SHEEP HUNT DEPOSITS: 50% at time of booking.

We accept Master Card and Visa
Video available for $25.00 (credited towards trip)

SHEEP HUNTING WITH STANLEY POTTS OUTFITTERS

In 1996, there were a total of 116 tags in Idaho. This is down from 212 4-year ago. There will probably be a few less in 1997. Definitely not a bright situation. However, I don't think our licensed areas will have any reductions. I think Rocky Mountain hunts 520-A2 and 526-1 will still have 6 tags each and 527L will have 3 California Bighorn hunts 741-1 and 741-2 will still have 5 tags each and 741-3 will have 3 for a total of 27 with 6 possible nonresident tags.

We took 2 rams for 4 hunters in 1996. One ram was missed and one hunter who did not show a ram.

We will still watch the drawing process for you at no charge except that we expect you to hunt with us if you draw. If you want to apply, send us a personal check made out to The Idaho Dept. of Fish and Game for $1007.50 which buys your nonrefundable hunting license at $101.50 and your refundable tag fee of $906. We will apply for the specie you want to hunt. Deadline is April 30, BUT, don't wait till the last minute - we live 58 miles from town and have twice a week mail service!

Get in sheep shape. You will have a better chance at a ram plus the hunt will be much more enjoyable. We will send you a separate gear list for sheep hunt after you draw.

SHEEP REFERENCES

Holton Quinn (208) 756-4661	Greg Dixon (501) 489-58?
Ron Rock (208) 772-8168	Glen Thurman (214) 286-63?
Bob Boucher (617) 595-1439	David Mode (404) 992-78
Dennis Gratton (208) 342-0360	Barbara Sackman (516) 883-39?
Chuck Lohr (208) 342-0360	Kevin Moore (619) 598-19?

DEER & ELK REFERENCES

Tom Schueth (402) 379-3041	Monte Mahon (509) 924-77
John Pennings (402) 777-9420	David Prantner (507) 437-15
Tom Archer (916) 587-2801	Tom Bowen (402) 423-26

1994 Auction Tag Buyer - Glen Thurman, Midland, Texas

Steve McIvor, Bellingham, WA

Tom Schueth, Norfolk, Nebraska - His first bull!

David Prantner, Austin, MN

Erik Brook, Reno, Nevada

Bob Boucher, Linn, MA

David Mode, Roswell, Georgia

RECOMMENDED GEAR LIST FOR HUNTING TRIPS:

Big Game Rifle (sighted in for 200 yards) you are familiar with and can handle, plus 40 rounds of cartridges. Use proven loads and bullets that will hold together when they hit.

Enough meat sacks or game bags to hold 4 quarters of elk meat plus 2 for deer. Binoculars - Waterproof match container - Insect repellant.

Good pocket knife. (Belt knife in good scabbard is okay. I prefer the folding models.)

Fanny pack or small day pack. (For lunches, snacks, flashlight, camera, etc.)

Small flashlight. (Pocket model with extra batteries and bulb.)

Small camera and extra film. Extra eyeglasses if you wear them and sunglasses if you need them for snow or glare.

Small overnight bag with towel, washcloth, soap, chapstick, toothbrush and any prescriptions.

Good sleeping bag. If you want to bring air mattresses, okay.

One pair leather gloves and one pair warm gloves or mittens.

Good set of rain gear or poncho. Preferably green or camouflage color. (The plastics tear.)

Well broken-in leather hunting boots with Vibram soles, plus, 1 pair slippers or tennis shoes.

Two pairs wool or felt insoles. Four changes light wool socks. Four changes nylon or silk socks.

Hunting hat or cap with visor and earmuffs. Wool pullover cap. Three pair light long johns. Three pair undershorts. Several T-shirts or undershirts. Two or three pairs light wool pants and overalls. Light wool jacket and four hunting shirts.

AFTER APPROXIMATELY OCTOBER 15 ADD THE FOLLOWING GEAR:

Heavy wool coat, wool pants and wool socks. Heavy long johns. Insulated pacs with Vibram or comparable soles.

Please feel free to adjust this list up or down to your own preference but you should be able to get everything but your rifle into one or two canvas duffle bags with a total weight of approximately 60#.

We will furnish foam pads and cots for sleeping and rifle scabbards if you need them.

If you have any dietary or food preferences beyond normal camp fare, please let us know.

RULES OF THE HUNT:

1. All rifle chambers unloaded on horses and in camp. (Bullets okay in magazine.) Have a few shells available on your person for the trip in. It's a big advantage for the game when we run into them on the trail and everybody's bullets are mantled up and packed on some mule. Please tape rifle muzzle to keep barrel clear.
2. All rifle chambers unloaded while walking trails.
3. Rifle chambers to be loaded after dismounting from horse if game is jumped, on the actual stalk or with the guide while bugling. (EXTREME CARE WHILE CHAMBER IS LOADED!)
4. While hunting or making a stalk, walk in your guides EXACT footsteps and approximately 4-6 feet back.
5. Keep all noises to a minimum. Voices, rattling bullets, metallic clanking, coughing, or the sound of frozen pant cuffs rubbing together - any of these at the wrong time could spook game.
6. Dismount and mount from the uphill side of your horse in steep country unless we tell you differently. (We walk and lead horses on downhill trails to rest them and allow your legs to limber up.) If possible, always use some sort of rest while shooting. LESS MISSED AND CRIPPLED ANIMALS.
7. Get your legs and lungs in shape to walk a few mountain miles. It will make your hunt more enjoyable plus enhance your chances of a successful hunt.

We are members of Idaho Outfitters and Guide Association, The Foundation for North American Wild Sheep, The Grand Slam Club #160, The Rocky Mountain Elk Foundation, North American Outfitters Association, Safari Club, North American Hunting Club and America Outdoors. We are also life members of The National Rifle Association. We have 39 years outfitting experience.

Our licensed area is approximately 50 square miles in Unit 20-A of the Frank Church River of No Return Wilderness Area. It is on the west side of the Middle Fork of the Salmon River in the Salmon National Forest. Our California bighorn area is in Unit 41.

Our base camp is at Colson Creek and can be reached by car. It is approximately a 7 hour ride to the first camps. The hunting area includes Color Creek, Nolan Creek, Reese Creek, Cradle Creek, Nugget Creek, Stoddard Creek and Papoose Creek.

I needed a horn chandelier and couldn't afford one so I built my own with antlers from elk Joy and I had taken.

Ken Johnson by our Cessna 180 2242C.

Stan Potts and Jim Renshaw present Idaho Governor Cecil Andrus a plaque after his mule wiped him out.

The sorrel mule on the left and the pinto horse on the right were both killed by falls down the mountain on this trip. Photo courtesy Chris Hendren.

This bull's skull had split, probably from a fight. The right horn grew out of the side of his head. Stan Potts found this head.

Holton Quinn and Stan Potts draw water from a cliff-side spring while on a sheep hunt. Photo courtesy Brian Edgerton.

A weird elk antler, evidently one where the horn grows from both pestles, and then 90 degrees off one side. This set of antlers was found by Wilde Brough.

Chapter 15

SNOW BLIND

I'd heard about people going snow blind but never really gave it much thought. I figured that you'd have to be pretty dumb to allow it to happen to you.

Sure enough, and it affects you, I assume, for the rest of your life as it is still a major factor for me at age sixty-eight and counting. I was about twenty-four when it happened to me.

It happened on a deer hunt in Nevada. We had received a nice

Stan Potts and famous sheep outfitter Jess Taylor with seven of the nine rams taken in 1968. Idaho had a total harvest of 36 that year.

snowfall of about a foot the night before and there was a thick blanket of fog when daylight came.

I left the ranch in Clover Valley alone in my old Jeep and drove Southeast past Snow-water Lake and Point Springs to Spruce Mountain. It was probably about forty or fifty miles by dirt roads.

I got around to the east side of the mountain and drove up a long canyon as far as the Jeep would go. It was still foggy when I parked the Jeep about 10 a.m. and started walking up the canyon.

It looked like the fog was thinner above me and that as I climbed in elevation I would get above it where I could see and look for a big Mule Deer buck.

I had just traded for a .308 Ruger automatic rifle and was packing it. I had watched the guy I had gotten it from kill a deer with it but I had never shot it myself.

Pretty soon I climbed up out of the cold dreary fog and into beautiful warm sunlight. As far as the eye could see it was an unbroken sea of white! Not as much as a dark spot of rocks, trees, sagebrush or anything.

After climbing another hour or so up the canyon I spotted a lone buck with good horns.

Harry Robinson and his 34-inch mule deer buck on the hood of my Jeep® that I was driving on the trip where I went snow blind.

He was standing across the canyon about three hundred yards away. I found a good rest by brushing the snow from the top of a rock about three feet high and anchored myself for the shot that would drop the buck.

I placed the crosshairs about three inches under the top of his chest and squeezed the trigger.

He never even moved!

Now, I had with me three full clips plus some loose shells making a total of twenty cartridges.

With the deep snow there was no way to see where my bullets were hitting.

I raised it above him and shot again. No reaction whatsoever from the deer. I kept shooting. I lowered it dead center – below his chest – to the right – to the left.

After most of the shells were gone the deer still didn't have a clue that he was being hunted and supposed to be dead!

He just stood there and listened to the pop of my rifle.

When I was down to one bullet – I took it out of my rifle and put it in my pocket. I waved so-long to the deer and headed back down the canyon toward the Jeep.

I had been in the bright, sunny, white landscape for several hours and as I followed my tracks back I noticed that I had to squint a lot. The snow was taking on a pinkish hue that kept getting darker pink and then moved towards red.

Eventually, I could not see, plus I could not stand the burning pain of opening my eyes!

I finally got my waterproof match container out of my pocket. I undid it by feel, got a match out, struck it and let it burn till it got hot on my fingers. I blew it out and when it cooled, I rubbed the ash under each eye.

In a few minutes by opening my eyes a tiny bit, and looking for a split second, I could memorize the tracks and terrain enough to make a few steps.

By burning a few more matches and darkening my cheeks as much as I could and making a few steps at a time, I was able to get back to the Jeep in the next few hours.

A slow drive home doing the same think but as darkness came I could see pretty well.

The problem then was a splitting headache and still horribly burning eyes.

To this day, under similar circumstances of snow or water glare, it starts back. I have to have dark glasses available before the dreaded pink color starts to build. I know the snow blindness is ready to return if I don't stop it.

BIG BULL, BIG BUCKS AND NO MEAT TO PACK!

Along about 1955 Joy and I teamed up with some neighbors to organize the yearly elk hunt.

The initial group this year started out with Gerald Twitchell, Stan Johnson, Joy and myself. We planned to go back into the Stoddard Creek country to see if we could capture some winters meat.

Gerald had the most horses and mules to put into the community pack string but as usual, some, no most of them had a problem or two.

One of them named Brownie had a tendency to kick, as in dangerous, kick your head off, type of kicking. He had kicked Gerald in the face the year before and eliminated most of Gerald's front teeth.

We took two truck loads, probably around twelve of fourteen head, down to the mouth of the Middle Fork of the Salmon River where the pack bridge crosses the Salmon.

There we ran into a couple of mutual friends that had come down the river to go hunting also. There plan was to hire one of the boatman like Don Smith to take them down the river to hunt.

The leader of this pair was Jay Beus from Challis and his long-time sheep ranch foreman that will hereafter be referred to as the "Basco".

Jay had just sold his sheep outfit and this trip was supposed to be a bonus for the foreman to reward him for his many years of helping Jay build one of the best sheep outfits in Idaho. (Known as the Drake Place, The Rogers Place, The Beus Place and the Ingram Place in Round Valley south of Challis, Idaho.)

However, when Jay saw us he propositioned us to take the foreman along with our group and Jay would go back to Salmon and celebrate the ranch sale while he waited for us. Elk hunting was not high on Jay's priority list!

Jay had a brand new pickup and he had purchased and loaded it with fine gourmet foods for his planned boat trip. He told us, "Get in there and take what you want."

So, our usual fare of beans, rice and raisins, stews and the sourdough jug had the addition of canned hams, canned oysters, sardines, kippered herring, French bread, fine wines and whiskey, (Lots of whiskey!)

The sourdough jug however, remained an important tool in this little pilgrimage in spite of a near catastrophe orchestrated by one of the knuckle-headed horses, named Anny, and yours truly.

I was leading three or four of these semi-broke refugees from a mustang band and part of my cargo was the precious sourdough crock.

In one of my many spectacular wrecks the first morning, the sour dough jug got broken. No, not cracked, badly broken! Probably fifteen or twenty odd shaped ceramic pieces in the bottom of a pannier mixed up with the sourdough starter. The ultimate puzzle!

That evening one of the greatest back country repair jobs of all time took place. We separated the pieces from the sourdough and rebuilt the crock, being careful to keep a film of dough between each piece. Sort of like mortar between bricks.

When it was back together we cut a piece of a gunny sack, (burlap bag), to go around the crock and rubbed a film of sourdough on it before wrapping it around the crock and tying it with string.

We barely had enough starter left to keep it going but our welding job worked and the jug came out of the mountains with us. It was kind of hard to abandon the masterpiece after all it had been through!

When we had arrived at the North Fork of Stoddard Creek to set up camp a couple more interesting events materialized.

We had two sacks of whole oats on the aforementioned Brownie. He was tied to a tree while we were unpacking the rest of the string when, who knows why, a typical mountain commotion developed.

Brownie succeeded in breaking both sacks of oats open, tearing the packsaddle apart and off and breaking his halter apart and tearing up the mountain completely free!

Twitchell, this creature's illustrious owner, was quick to point out Brownie's merits.

Best horse we've got. "Feeds all the other horses, unsaddles himself and turns himself loose. It's pretty hard to find a horse that good!"

We got the rest of the stock unpacked, caught Brownie, and had everything tied up while trying to get camp set up.

The Basco, wanting to help, was aimed into the forest to retrieve some dry wood for camp.

Remember Brownie, once again, practically hunts down people to kick. We looked up and here comes the Basco about a yard from Brownies hind feet and dragging a twenty foot dry tree with limbs slapping Brownie on the legs and ribs. Brownie just stood there and shook!

I guess it's time to tell why we called him the Basco.

That evening after supper and planning the next day's hunt he informed us that he had never had a hunting license.

When he and Jay planned their trip they decided he would borrow one of the Basque sheepherder's license and tags. Not very legal but that was the situation.

Some Basque names are pretty long and hard to pronounce and the name on the license was one of the longest.

I don't remember it for sure but let's call it something like Dominiko Archebuletta. Kind of hard to pronounce and harder to remember.

We told him, "Man, Mike Wilkins, the game warden, spends a lot of time back here patrolling for poachers. If he shows up, he will check all our licenses and you will have to be able to remember and pronounce your name.

"We will help you by asking your name when you are least expecting it to help get you prepared."

Poor guy, practiced for a week and when we left he couldn't pronounce his name!

He did turn out to be pretty handy though.

Because he didn't know who he was and couldn't hunt, he became our horse mover. We would ride out a few miles and he would bring the horses back to camp so the rest of us could hunt back afoot. A couple of these excursions had great amounts of excitement for Joy and I.

BIG BULL

The first day of hunting we all went together to the top of the mountain to the west of Stoddard Point.

Joy and I got off at what we now call Wolf Point. Those of you that have been up there since the Canadian wolves were turned loose know where it is.

Gerald and Stan would go on another mile, The Basco would take the horses back down and the rest of us would hunt down the mountain afoot.

Joy and I dropped down a few hundred feet in elevation and

probably a thousand yards in distance when we came upon a VERY fresh bull bed.

The bull had gotten up and urinated in his bed and the bubbles were still standing around the spot. That's what you call fresh!

I looked around and from the opposite side of a huge fir tree protruded the lasts three points of an antler that I suspected from the size was attached to a giant bull!

We were about three feet from the tree and the bull was about three feet on the opposite side.

I pointed to the horn and motioned to her that I would step around the tree and shoot him. We would have a "powder burned" elk to show off, right?

I had an old army Springfield O3-A3 .30-06 rifle with no safety. You either had to lift the handle on the bolt or pull the bolt back to cock it. Either way was far too noisy a maneuver for hunting elk at nine feet!

When I cocked it and it clicked the horn whirled, I jumped around the tree and the bull was running straight away toward the bottom of a little gulch and yes, he was BIG. I didn't want to take a "Texas heart shot" so I passed. The other side of the gulch was open but the bottom was treed. I just knew he would turn down the bottom with cover instead of going up the open hillside.

I told Joy, "Come on, we can head him off and get a shot".

Guess what, the bull crossed the little gulch and went up the open hillside except now we had all these big trees blocking our view and couldn't see him!

Anyway, only one of the many times I have miss-guessed the actions of one of God's mountain creatures.

BIG BUCK NUMBER ONE

There was a couple inches of fresh snow and as we got further down the mountain and into the lodgepole pines there were lots of down trees and you had to step on some of them to keep going.

My feet slipped on one and I fell backwards cracking my head on a log and knocking myself pretty silly.

After a short while the cobwebs cleared and we moved down to a little opening and decided to eat our lunches.

About one hundred and fifty yards below us and on the opposite side of the gulch was an uprooted tree with roots protruding in all directions. We both remarked how much it looked like a giant set of mule deer horns except for being too big.

Neither of us had any binoculars back in those days. If we had, this story may have had a different ending.

When we finished our sandwiches and stood up to continue down the hill our uprooted tree jumped up and disappeared down the mountain!

It was a buck of astronomical proportions! One of those that you dream about. Tines in all directions and wide as an ox-yoke. Oh well. What might have been.

How big? Who knows. But, Boyd Thietten and his son Jay were hunting in there a year or so later and Jay killed a many pointed buck that I have heard stories of forty-two to forty-seven inches wide. Whatever, that was probably our "uprooted tree"!

BIG BUCK NUMBER TWO

One tale shouldn't have two big bucks that got away but, "What the Hell," this one does.

Joy had borrowed my dad's lever action .308 rifle. It will hereafter be known as the "lever action automatic."

Joy and I took a few horses and went up to Stoddard Lookout and spent the day hunting. When we got there we were greeted by a small herd of mountain sheep ewes and lambs bedded all around the lookout. The only other creatures seen in the early part of the day was a forked-horn mule deer buck that decided we shouldn't be on his mountain. He would come up to us and stomp his feet as much as to say, "Get out of here, this is my domain!" Pretty cute.

We decided to head back down to camp that afternoon. As we got on the switchbacks above Stoddard Creek, another giant buck came running up the hill chasing some does. He was not much more than a hundred yards away and in pretty open country.

Joy grabbed the .308 out of her scabbard and started shooting but in the ensuing melee my horse got away with my gun and all the horses went galloping down the mountain.

I got back to Joy just as she shot the last bullet from her gun. Big buck is still chasing the does. He is unaware of the nearby danger. (Probably poor terminology as you will shortly see!)

I said, "Give me that rifle and some bullets so I can kill that big

S.O.B."

He was a perfect four-point and nearly as wide as the giant non-typical of a few days prior. Probably thirty-eight to forty inches on the spread but not too high.

I proceeded to reload the .308 after I had wrestled it and the bullets away from Joy and shot another volley into several points on the mountain where the buck wasn't.

By then he was too far up the mountain to shoot at and he had successfully avoided certain death.

That night back at camp Joy was telling the story and insisted she was able to keep firing without jacking the lever to reload the barrel. She had us so convinced that it was somehow a "lever action automatic" that we had to get the gun and try to convince her that she was unknowingly levering the new cartridge in without even realizing it.

Could we both have been plagued with the dreaded "Buck Fever"? Probably, but we did find out that rifle would never inherit the moniker, "Old Meat In The Pot!

WHITE CREATURE IN THE DARK

So far we had not been any great danger to the game populations on the Middle Fork. Hopefully we would be able to change this as shortly we would be forced to return to what is known as "The Other World." It was going to be a long winter with nothing to flavor the soup if our luck didn't improve.

On one of our final days of the hunt, Joy and I went back up to Stoddard Lookout and looped down around the head of Nugget Creek and went down the ridge between Nugget Creek and Cradle Creek. Probably didn't know the names of where we were back then as it wasn't too important. Now that we are outfitting in there it kind of impresses the clients if you can tell them where you are!

We tied up our horses on the ridge and dropped down on the Cradle Creek side part way to the creek and started hunting around the hill upstream to the West.

Two elk jumped up, a spike bull and a yearling cow. Choice flavoring for the soup plus primo meat in the steak department!

I was able to knock down the little bull across a small canyon. I told Joy to watch the spot where he had fallen until I got there because it was really brushy and I didn't want to lose him.

Pretty quick I found him and called Joy to come on over. When she got there she had another interesting story.

Unbeknownst to me the cow was standing near where I was looking for the spike. I had a red earmuff cap on, the kind that the earmuffs tie over the top or under your chin when it is cold. They were untied and kind of flopping around on top of the cap.

Joy saw the elk and pulled her gun up on it. Then it moved and I came into view in nearly the same spot. She said the floppy eared cap looked so much like the cows head in the brush that she couldn't keep track of which was which. Therefore the cow got away, but, so did I!

I told her to go get the horses while I cleaned and split the elk to pack. That way we could get headed back a little quicker. It was now late afternoon and it would be dark in a couple hours.

I finished my butchering job and sat down on a log and lit a smoke while I was waiting for her.

When I finished there was no noise of the horses coming so I headed to the top of the ridge to help her.

When I got to the horses they were still tied up and alone. No Joy! I walked out where I could see down the ridge and could see her headed towards the Middle Fork. She had missed the horses and was over a mile down the ridge and going in the wrong direction.

I yelled to turn her around and when she got back we took the horses down and loaded a half elk split length wise on each of our riding saddles. We led them into the bottom off Cradle Creek to head back up and over the top and back down to our camp.

By now it was pitch black and I had never been up that canyon.

I had great night vision back in those days which was a good thing as we had no flashlights.

After about a half hour of working our way up the canyon I looked up ahead of me and there was a white-animal type object.

I would stop and we would look trying to decide what it was. We would move forward and it would move out of sight. Then it would show up again still moving ahead of us.

The horses were not scared and we could not hear it move.

I finally got some matches out of my pocket and kneeled down and struck them trying to make out some kind of track. Nothing that I could see. This went on for several minutes and probably a couple hundred yards. After that we never saw it again.

About thirty minutes later we came through the middle of Sandy Brook's, the local outfitter, camp. It was now about midnight and the camp was dark.

From here on was a horse trail and we made it back to camp with no problems.

The white creature? No idea. It appeared to be about the size of a mountain goat, but under those conditions that's a wild guess, plus I think the horses would have been more agitated.

A white mule or burro – maybe. But still no noise and no inquisitive horses.

Another of life's little mysteries – unknown and unsolved.

Another little side note here. Where we were camped at the bottom of Grassy was where Frank Lantz told me that he had been sent in there by the Forest Service to do a survey on the bighorn sheep. He didn't tell me the year but obviously in their early years.

From one spot on Middle Grassy he had over four hundred bighorn sheep in sight at one time! He said he couldn't get a better count than that because sheep were going out of sight in some places and coming into sight in others. That would have been a sight to dream about!

THE ALBINO LAMBS

When we were coming back thru Nolan Creek headed down toward the river we had another white creature (creatures) experience.

I was in the lead when a small herd of mountain sheep came across the trail ahead of me. In the bunch were two snow white lambs!

One's mother was a young thrifty ewe. The other's mother was very old and very decrepit. It was a bright sunny day and the lambs would walk either in the shade of their mothers or with their heads right in the ewes flanks. There were several other normal colored lambs in the bunch.

The old ewes lamb got separated from her in some mountain maple and elderberry bushes and just stood there bleating.

Joy walked up to within about five feet and took a picture. That is when we realized they were albinos and why they couldn't see in the bright sun.

She said, "Should I catch it and help it around the bushes?" I said, "No, I'm afraid its mother might abandon it. Just back away and we will see what happens."

Finally, the old ewe got back around the bushes and by her marooned baby, it got its' head under her flank on the shady side and they were able to work back into the bunch.

Amazingly, the whole herd had waited for the reunion before they moved on around the mountain. It was probably the normal ritual and they somehow knew the little white guys were different and needed all the help they could get.

Interesting sidelight: Mike Wilkins, the game warden, and his wife Cal had come thru this country a couple of weeks before.

Cal was in the lead when she came upon the sheep herd with the white lambs.

She hollered back, "Mike, there are two baby mountain goats with these mountain sheep!

That's what they looked like – baby mountain goats. And that little canyon is now known as Albino Creek.

In a lifetime in the mountains and looking at lots of mountain sheep I have only seen two Albinos and they were in the same herd! Why? Who knows?

1. PITTSBURGH PIRATES SHEEP HUNT

When we were outfitting out of the Taylor Ranch on lower Big Creek in what was then called the Idaho Primitive Area we got to do a lot of sheep hunting. This was the period in 1960s'.

There was no draw on sheep until about 1970 so sheep hunters could just buy a tag and come hunting. It was possible to have a pretty large group of friends come on a sheep hunt and all of them have a tag in their pocket.

In about 1968 we had four hunters, including Dan Galbreath, one of the owners of the Pittsburgh Pirates. The Vice-President of the Pirates, Bob Edler, Mr. Galbreath's attorney, Richard Brentlinger, and Dr. Bill Rigsby rounded out the group.(Interesting sidenote: I had been running strictly from memory on some of these stories and did not remember Dr. Bill Rigsby's name. His son went through Salmon and bought one of the Pott's Factor books because he recognized my name. He showed it to his dad and Bill wrote me a letter and ordered a couple books for himself and Bob Edler!)

I had two head guides Dick Hall and Fay Detweiler at one our sheep camps along with my wife, Joy, and two apprentice guides, Jim Quintana and Larry Ledenski. Joy would be the cook and sheep spotter and everyone else would look for sheep while I went to the ranch-airstrip to pick up the hunters who were being brought in by airplane.

Unbeknownst to me the hunters had decided to play a trick on me. Remember, I had never met any of these guys. Just letters and phone calls had made the trip arrangements.

The trick was supposed to work as follows: When they all got off the airplane they were going to all act like they were homosexuals!

The attorney, Richard Brentlinger, was the president of The Worlds Weightlifters Association. His biceps muscles were probably at least nineteen inches around and the rest of his body was muscles on top of muscles.

The flight into the Taylor Ranch Strip for people that are not used to mountain flying can be somewhat exciting with blind approaches and rocks not to far from either wingtip.

The flight had evidently unnerved most of the members of the group and all but one of them had forgotten the trick they were going to play on

The Pittsburgh Pirates crew, Bob Edler, Dick Brentlinger and Dan Galbraeth.

old Potts!

Guess which one remembered the trick? Yeah! Brentlinger the muscle man!

He got off the plane and walked up to me and with the sweetest, syrupy whisper you could imagine he greeted me with, "Hi Stan, My friends call me Rickey"!

I had already met the rest of the crew and after Brentlingers' introduction they fessed up on their little plan and I heaved a giant sigh of relief!

On the way into camp that evening we stopped just after Sundown to glass across the canyon for rams and Dan spotted four nice rams.

We went on in to camp and after a nice supper that Joy had ready we went to bed dreaming of the morrows' hunt.

We woke up to a rain-snow-sleet storm with about one hundred feet of visibility. It kept storming until the afternoon of the fourth day.

We could then use the binoculars and spotting scopes and relocated the rams. They were in the thick trees and in a poor place to try a stalk so we just bided our time for a couple more days.

While keeping track of them as best we could in the trees they all came running around the mountain at a full bore run. Behind them was another big ram chasing them out of his domain. They finally stopped, all had a big bunch of head butting and bedded down as a group.

Now we had five rams if we could ever get them settled down in a spot where I felt we could stalk them.

We were about a hard three hour stalk to get where they were.

Late one afternoon with not much over three hours of daylight left the rams were in a pretty good spot and I decided to try them with Galbreath and Brentlinger.

The rams were in pretty cliffy terrain and we had to come in from the side to get where we might have a shot.

We got up close to where they were when I heard the dreaded rocks rolling, the sound of running rams – not what you want to hear but they were below us and the evening thermals were now down mountain and they had winded us.

The guys could have gotten a running shot at the smallest ram of the five but I held them off and told them we would relocate the rams and try again.

We had to go back down one mountain and up another in the dark to get back to our camp. Dick Brentlingers' knees went out real badly

We had a four-day wait on this hunt before we made the stalk, and then I blew it! From left are Dan Galbraeth, Bill Rigsby, Stan Potts and Dick Brentlinger.

because they just couldn't pack all that weight in that type of terrain. We manufactured some makeshift crutches from limbs so that he could make it to camp. He just had to lay around for the next few days to get the swelling out of his knees.

The next day the rest of us took horses to the top of the mountain the rams had headed over, probably four or five thousand feet up. My plan was to try and find their tracks in the rocks and attempt to follow and find them again.

We were able to do this except that Bob Edler felt he wouldn't be able to go down the mountain on the other side the several thousand feet it looked like the rams had gone.

Galbreath and I started down the mountain following the ram tracks as best we could but at least keeping ourselves in the right direction between sightings of tracks.

About two thousand feet down the mountain I came to a cliff and carefully looked over. The rams were bedded under the cliff with the ram that had chased the other four partially behind a tree – with no shot until he stood up.

The spot we had to shoot from was not big enough for both of us to watch from. I usually get to be a nervous wreck in these types of situations. There is no way to tell what will happen when you have to trust the hunter to make the right decisions, shoot the right ram, don't take a chance on shooting through one and hitting another, waiting for the right shot, etc.

However, Galbreath was one of the most knowledgeable hunters I have ever been with, so knowledgeable in fact that I learned a lot about hunting from him. He had hunted Africa several times and had picked the native guide's brains and actions as he hunted with them. He had learned to start a fire with the bow and stick method. He said the natives would watch for a big pile of dry elephant dung for tinder and would sit down and build a fire just to light their cigarettes! I was pretty impressed as much trouble as I can have building a fire with my dry matches, pitch wood and cigarette lighter.

Anyway, Dan looked over the cliff and whispered to me. "Don't

Dan Galbraeth, owner of the Pittsburgh Pirates baseball team at the time of this hunt. He and his family have had three horses from their "Darby Dan Farms" win the Kentucky Derby. Chateaugay in 1963 and Proud Clarion in 1967 were the first two.

worry, I know the right ram and when he stands up and gives me a shot, I'll take him."

A couple hours later he pulled the rifle up and shot. He then turned to me with the thumbs up sign.

We both peered over the cliff to see what was going on. The big ram was laying in his bed and all the other rams were standing with their noses touching his body. As he stiffened and slowly stretched his legs while dying, they spooked and run for a few seconds. Then all became very quiet. We couldn't see what was happening because of the thick trees and the shape of the mountain.

We waited about thirty minutes and then couldn't stand it any more. We had to go down and see our ram.

When we got to the ram, all the other rams were lying down about fifty yards away and were nearly oblivious to us. I could see the other big ram and whispered to Dan, "I don't have any idea if this will work but I will go back to the top and see if I can find Bob and get him back down

Stan Potts and sheep ribs. The guys said in all their sheep hunts, they had never gotten to have sheep rib barbecue. Accordingly, we found some mountain mahogany, built a fire for some good coals and about midnight we had our sheep rib barbecue. Umm, good!

here."

I went back to the top, found Bob and the other two guides, and we all went most of the way back down. I left the two guides about where Dan had shot the ram from and I took Bob down to where Dan was laying behind a log.

He had drawn a map in the dust with the location of each of the other rams. He told Bob, "When you ease your gun over the log the big one is the furthest away and looking away from us."

Bang! Two hours after the first ram was shot we had been lucky enough to get the other big ram. (See Horse Mountain Sheep Horns-story, page 83 of *The Pott's Factor versus Murphy's Law* for the ending of this hunt.)

Stan Potts says of this caricature of him drawn by his good friend Tom Archer, "The Truckee Barrister," and used in this book with Archer's permission, that "this really brings one down to size." He also noted that the permission agreement is 26 pages long!

Chapter 16

Bar Stories – San Francisco and Chicago

Through the years of traveling around to promote and establish our outfitting business, I had a couple of interesting and heretofore unpublished bar experiences.

The first materialized like this. We were in San Francisco at the Sports and Boat show held at the Cow Palace. There was a little bar on the corner where we would occasionally take and afternoon break and have a beer or two with past or potential customers.

In the afternoon it was just a normal beer bar with a mixed clientele of white, black, and Spanish customers. I had never been there in the evening and the first time I went there I received a rude awakening.

We had been to a dinner party with some friends in Los Altos and were returning to our motel room near the Cow Palace. I decided to stop at our little bar a get a six-pack of beer.

When I walked into the bar, which was filled with probably over one hundred patrons, I realized I was the only white person in the establishment! It was populated with black people only and most of them were looking at the big-hatted cowboy that had just entered. Me!

I ordered a six-pack of beer and noticed that one of the patrons was staring directly at me as the bartender was getting my order.

When the bartender sat my beer on the plank he said, "That guy would like to buy you a drink."

I just told him, "No thanks," as I had to leave.

Bartender relays the message. Large black gentleman gets off his stool probably ten seats down the bar and ambles back to where I am standing. (Quite nervously, I might add!)

I'm thinking I've been in many much more comfortable situations than this one.

He holds out his hand to shake hands which I gladly do.

He says,"Where you all out of?"

I answered, "Nevada and Idaho."

He comes back with, "Man, I drive through there and I need some tickets to the sport show."

Ordinarily I had a pocket-full but had given them all away at the dinner party. (I guarantee you I would have given quite a bit of money for a few right at that moment!) I explained my predicament but was not really getting through to him.

Once again, "Hey man, Go to your boot and get me some tickets!"

At this juncture I probably did one of my best jobs of salesmanship of all time!

I told him, "Hey man, (we were hey-manning this conversation to death). You stop by the Idaho Outfitters booth when you come to the show tomorrow, I'll have a bunch of tickets for you man, and we will go have a drink."

Sounded good to him. We shook hands again and I walked out with my six-pack of beer feeling I had "dodged a bullet" **Magnum Size!**

Major tough job the next day watching every black man that even came close to the outfitters booth and trying to remember what the one I was going to give the tickets to looked like!

He never came by.

Chicago – The Amphitheater

In Chicago the Idaho Outfitters Association kept a booth, to be used at the shows there, stored with one of Norm and Bill Guth's hunter clients.

Whoever went back on a given year would pick it up and set it up and re-store it at the end of the show.

On this particular year Jack Nygaard and I were part of the crew, along with Ted Epley and Martin Capps.

Jack and I ran out of Copenhagen late one Friday afternoon and walked across the street from the stockyards-amphitheater complex to a bar to buy a couple of cans.

It was payday and, as in San Francisco, the bar was inhabited by several hundred black guys celebrating Friday afternoon. The only white people were the three lady bartenders and Nygaard and me in our cowboy hats.

It's amazing how quiet several hundred celebrating people can get when two big-hatted cowboys enter their secluded haven!

And that's a lot of eyeballs when they are all aimed your way. It seemed like hours for the bartender to get our cans of "chewbacky" and for us to exit their domain! In reality, it was probably a couple minutes. Probably the longest couple minutes you can imagine and it took a couple of big chews to settle our nerves.

This string was led by one man – a string with over 45 head!

Chapter 17

Mule Days

In the early days of our outfitting career one of the highlights each year was attending the Sports and Boat Show at the Cow Palace in San Francisco to promote our business

Several outfitters from the Idaho Outfitters Association would attend and take turns working the Idaho booth to try and encourage people to come to Idaho for hunting, fishing and boating trips.

Also attending the show was a group called the "High Sierra Packers". They had a small packstring in their booth and it was easy to locate from the braying of the "Mountain Canaries".

Joy and I got to know several of the packers and their wives and listened to their promotion of the "Mule Days" in Bishop, California, each Spring.

Being a "Mule Whacker," I decided we had to go see it firsthand.

When we arrived the first day, we just bought tickets and sat in the bleachers because all the grandstand seating was sold out. It got pretty hot up there at the top of the bleachers with no shade.

On one of my trips to the beer stand (only to try to combat the heat, mind you), I ran into some of the people we had met from the "High Sierra Packers". These people were in charge of the entire "Mule Days" production.

They asked me where we were sitting and I told them, "Up at the top of the bleachers".

They immediately had me go get Joy and escorted us to the Grandstand – front and center, first row – a neat little area, partitioned off, with about eight padded seats and tables for your drinks. It was labeled, "Governors' Box!"

I said, "Man we can't sit here. What if the Governor shows up?" (Concern about the Potts' Factor was lurking in the back of my mind).

Their reply was, "He is not coming and the box is yours for the balance of the "Mule Days"

So, that is what we did. You can get pretty good pictures when you have the best seat in the house!

And, it is great watching the neighboring spectators craning their necks and trying to figure out who the two important celebrities occupying the Governors' Box are!

The "Traveling Bar! This is a position of importance.

Monty Montana performing.

A 20-mule hitch at a dead run!

An authentic antique reproduction of an ox yoke. (Okay, a phoney!) I wanted one and couldn't afford it, so I built several to sell – and still do!

Chapter 18

Mustanging

THE SHORTY PRUNTY HORSE CATCH

Through the years of knocking around the West and being involved in the ranching, outfitting and cowboying world, I have seen and been involved with some unique instances of certain individuals being able to exhibit remarkable equine control.

I'm sure some of these instances were the forerunner of the current methods of equine training that are geared strongly to the ability of the trainers to utilize and focus their training on the horses' and mules' mental capacity. The ultimate results of this method are horses and mules that do the things the trainer strives for without being exposed to the "bronc stompers" training method. (See my rendition of Wiley Carrols' fast horse training method in *"The Pott's Factor Versus Murphy's Law"*, p. 45)

One instance that genuinely impressed me had to do with a friend of mine from northern Nevada named Shorty Prunty.

Shorty and his brother, Corky, and father, Earl, and families had ranches and range permits in the general area of the high desert, mountain country of northern Nevada/southern Idaho with their ranching headquarters located at Charleston, Nevada. This country was and still is what could be described as "exceedingly remote" without stretching the description at all. Mail came in the winter-time about sixty miles by Super Cub that dropped the incoming mail by the ranch house and picked the outgoing mail up between two small towers with a hook and cable arrangement. This definitely is the ultimate description of the Post Service motto that "The Mail Must Go Through!"

The Prunty families operated like a lot of us in the ranching business did and still do to survive and, hopefully, make a buck or two – they diversified. Besides running a lot of horses and cattle to sell, they operated a guide service for the big mule deer bucks that inhabited northern Nevada and a lot of their horses were used in this part of the operation in the fall.

In 1958, Shorty, Corky, my father-in-law Lloyd Blume, Claude Gerber, Slim Saxton, myself, and several other guides and packers formed the "Elko County Guides and Packers Association." It was the forerunner of the present-day "Nevada Guides and Packers Association."

The first meeting was held at the Ranch Inn in Elko, Nevada, and I was elected Sergeant-at-Arms, which was a lot like being volunteered to cross a field of land mines.

Tensions and personality conflicts were at the forefront of the first meetings, until we were able to come together with some workable rules of operation that primarily delineated the areas of operation that each of us would use. I survived my "Sergeant-at-Arms" job and went on to be the president of both associations for a few years.

In addition to the cattle raising, horse raising, and guiding and packing, the Pruntys built up a fine rodeo string called the "Diamond A Rodeo Company." They started out producing amateur/semi-professional rodeos and then professional rodeos in what is now the P.R.C.A. The Diamond A Desert in southern Idaho/northern Nevada has, usually, pretty mild winters and most of the horses wintered out on the open range.

Now, towns in northern Nevada big enough to host any type of celebration, including a rodeo, are few and far between. The logistics of transporting a large string of bucking horses from the remote Charleston ranch to towns like Wells, Elko, Carlin and Battle Mountain prior to the use of large livestock hauling trucks was quite staggering. Back in those days, there weren't a great lot of ranch and drift fences so the horses were trotted overland from the ranch to the town where the rodeo would be held.

I will give you a scenario of the bucking horses arrival in the town of Wells, Nevada, because I am most familiar with that arrival. Picture a horse herd of sixty to eighty head coming out of the northwest on a trot of probably ten to fifteen miles per hour. In the lead is a cowboy riding a horse the herd will, hopefully, follow. Two or three other cowboys are in the rear and, along the flank, keeping the herd following and hoping they don't lose any in the huge dust cloud that envelops the herd. These are the times that you hoped for a rain storm to settle the dust or, the next best thing, a cross wind.

Otherwise, the guy in the lead couldn't see where to go with a tail wind or the guys on the drag couldn't see the herd with a head wind.

There were two railroad tracks to cross, the Southern Pacific and the Western Pacific. You could see the trains for several miles so could plan your crossings between trains.

Highway 40 was the only oiled road to cross back then with not too much traffic. When the dust cloud approached the highway from the northwest, a couple of cars would go out where they would be crossing and stop traffic. A few of the local ranchers and cowboys would go out on horseback to help get the stock on into the corrals at the rodeo arena. I competed as a cowboy on the Diamond A stock for a few years and then worked for the Pruntys as a flagmen, judge and later their rodeo announcer.

At the start of this story I was focused on feats of impressive horse training. I promise I will get back to at least one of those before this story is over.

One year Corky Prunty and his sons got a contract from the Bureau of Land Management to round up wild horses and mustangs from a large area where the mustangs were getting overpopulated and eating themselves out of house and home.

This was prior to the days of "Wild Horse Annie" and the government agencies and the ranchers with range permits could have some control over the mustang populations.

Corky hired me to do the airplane work by helping move the bands of mustangs a few miles to where Corky and the boys would be waiting on horseback to haze the horses into fenced fields and corrals to be sorted and sold.

Some of the better stock would be used for saddle and pack horses with the occasional one being a good enough bucking horse to make the bucking string.

Now back to the impressive horse training job by Shorty Prunty. One spring Shorty called me to hire me and my little one and a half ton Dodge stock truck to go with him to Oneil Basin and Vance Agees' ranch to pick up a couple of horses that had been lost from the rodeo string.

This northern Nevada country is big with mountain ranges, canyons and wide expanses of high desert grassland in between. Cattle and horses sometimes ended up on the neighboring ranges fifty to one hundred miles away.

Such was the case with these horses from the rodeo string. It had probably been a year or two (and maybe more) since the horses had even seen a human.

Horses in a rodeo string are generally thought of as wild, untrained, unmanageable creatures. "Right?"

We drove into Vance Agees' ranch and the two horses were together in a large corral probably one hundred and fifty feet across. Shorty got his lariat rope off the seat between us and walked into the corral.

He's going to rope each one so we can get them into the truck, "Correct?"

No, he made a small loop probably about two feet across as he held the loop in his right hand and walked to the center of the corral. The horses were standing and watching this part of the procedure unfold. Shorty stopped in the center of the corral, spoke to the horses and so help me, one of them walked across the corral and put his head into the loop! He led him over to where I was standing with a halter. We haltered him and Shorty walked back to the center of the corral, held the loop and the second horse walked over and put his head in the loop just like the first! Remember, these aren't pet horses! They are horses that for whatever reason ended up in the bucking string for bucking off the ranch cowboys or otherwise exhibiting unmanageable traits.

I tried to get Shorty to give me the secret but all I got was, "It's all in how you talk to them!"

I never did figure it out.

Prunty ranches are still in operation with Shorty's wife, Marge Bieroth Prunty, as the matriarch and ramrod of the outfit.

Frank "Shorty" Prunty and Harold "Corky" Prunty are both on the last big roundup.

HOW NOT TO BE A MUSTANGER

Northeast Nevada had a pretty high population of mustangs in the early years of my ranching days down there – in the late nineteen-fifties and early nineteen-sixties.

Read *"The Barnstorming Mustanger"* by Ted Barber for some insight into capturing wild horses during this period. The mustangs were worth a little money and were sorts of there for the taking. The 284-page book was published by Barber Industries out of Orovada, Nevada, in 1987 and can be found in many libraries across the West.

From the book's summary, we learn it is "a chronicle of one man's experiences in the West barnstorming in Oregon and rounding up more than 17,000, Yes, SEVENTEEN THOUSAND wild mustangs from the air in Nevada."

Ted Barber was one of those pilots that used an airplane as an extension of his mind and body.

Ted also flew for the Fish and Wildlife Service and the Nevada Department of Wildlife in the predator control program. I never did get to fly with him as a gunner, but three of my friends, Dick Hall, Bob Queroz and Eddie DeBernardi, did. They said his method of flying was uncanny. If they missed a coyote, he would pull the plane into a steep climb and watch the coyote out of the top of the canopy as he did a Chandelle and rolled the plane upright for another pass from the opposite direction, never or rarely losing sight of the coyote in the entire procedure.

This is a fun maneuver at several thousand feet. Ted was doing it for business at from twenty feet to two-hundred feet. Try it sometime!

He and Dick Hall would come by our house in Clover Valley, Nevada, about daylight when they were in the area hunting coyotes. Our house was two stories and Ted would come by at rooftop height to make sure I had the coffee pot on. He would land in my alfalfa field by the house, where we landed our Cessna 180, and they could come over for coffee and a bathroom call.

He showed me some of the innovations he had added to the plane for safety and practicality. He had very lightweight, colored strings taped to the fabric on the trailing edge of the wings. As the airplane speed was reduced towards a stall, the strings would not stay extended straight back from the wings in a crisp manner but would flutter and hang raggedly prior to the controls doing the same thing before a stall.

Another great innovation was his mounting the carburetor heat on the top of the control stick so you could apply and take off heat to the carburetor to control icing without removing the left hand from the throttle. The right hand could stay on the stick during tight maneuvers and the eyes could be focused on the business at hand.

He had other refinements, but these two are the ones I remember.

My salute to one of the great pilots!

However, sometimes the taking of these wild mustangs was not an easy task.

A lot of attempts to gather mustangs involved several neighbors, lots of saddle horses, lots of hard work building cedar post wings and corrals plus water traps to try to catch them on the water holes.

It usually boiled down to the ruining of some good saddle horses by their stepping in badger holes and falling in rocks and gullies to capture a few wild horses that weren't all that great after you caught them.

The mustangs were more like deer and elk than horses.

They pretty much went to the mountains during the day and come down into the valleys to graze just before dark. The mountains were mostly timbered with pinon' and juniper trees and other than with water traps they were nearly impossible to catch up there. You could glass them with binoculars and spotting scopes during the day from the valley floor. A lot of them would shade up in caves in pretty cliffy country.

Some of the valleys had a lot better wild horses than others.

Old-timers like Bob Steele had turned blooded remount stallions loose, so through the ensuing years some of these herds contained much better horses than the ordinary run of mustang. They all looked good running across the desert with manes and tails flying but sometimes after they were reduced to possession you wondered what attracted you to this big headed, slab sided, seven hundred pound sack of sand burrs!

In the course of helping move some of these horse herds with my airplane, I came up with the seemingly great plan. "You have heard this before. Correct?"

Tranquilizers as such had just become a method of handling wild animals such as mountain lions, bears, deer, elk etc.

All you have to do is inject the tranquilizer, wait for it to take effect, secure the animal and wait until it overcomes the effect of the drug. I planned on having some cowboys on horseback scattered along the desert floor to tie the mustangs down after the drug had taken effect.

I decided to make a trial run to work the bugs out of my system. I was already counting my money, as usual!

Oh, by the way, I was going to do the shooting of the tranquilizer darts from my Cessna 180 airplane!

In hazing the horses before I had just sort of ziz-zagged along behind them and changed their directions of travel from one hundred yards or so away or with a gallon can of rocks on a rope.

Now I had to get within a few feet to be able to place the dart from the airgun into said horse.

Here is how it didn't work!

When I would come up on a herd and get them lined out in a straight line in decent (as in semi-flat) country, I would then angle across the back end of the bunch at the necessary altitude, say fifteen or twenty feet, for the seemingly simple task of placing the dart in some horsehide.

Somehow, the sight and sounds of an airplane twenty or so feet long with thirty five feet wings coming over a wild horse herd at fifteen feet of altitude causes them to primarily not continue in a straight line! In fact, they can change directions eleven ways from Sunday and all in a seeming millisecond.

Flying the 180 with the door off and attempting to make this airgun/tranquilizer trick work proved far more difficult than I had envisioned.

Accordingly, it was filed under one more way to not to capture mustangs!

(See page 158, "The Mustang and the Snowmobile" story in *"The Pott's Factor Versus Murphy's Law"* for one of the many others.)

ROPING THE MUSTANG COLT

One year, about 1954, Don Brown and I left Mackay, Idaho, to go to a rodeo at Fort McDermott, Nevada. We were both trying to figure out how to make money at the rodeoing game and McDermott was the first rodeo of the season anywhere close to Mackay.

Don was in the bareback and saddle bronc riding and I was in the bareback, calf roping and team roping.

The first day of the two day rodeo Don made a beautiful bareback ride and was far in lead score-wise in the one go-round rodeo. I had just done mediocre in my attempts.

The next morning was a monsoon rain and by early afternoon they decided to cancel the rodeo. The rodeo committee then took all the prize money, including the entry fees, and gave it to the rodeo producer. Nothing we could do, so we headed back to Idaho.

We had my Ford nine passenger station wagon and were just starting up Golconda summit when a herd of mustangs ran across the road in front of us. Following behind was a very young colt. Don was driving and stopped the car. I grabbed my lariat, jumped out and impulsively roped the colt as he crossed the road following the herd.

Lariats have gotten me in trouble with bobcats, eagles, coyotes, etc. before so this was not the first impulse lashup!

What we were going to do with him I don't know. Probably haul him home in the back of the station wagon, raise him on a bottle and tell stories about the famous mustang, "Golconda", I guess.

No matter. About this time around the hillside following the horse herd in his Super Cub was the Lander County sheriff, Len Sheppard. From the way he was buzzing us in the airplane plus the colts' mother being none to happy, I turned him loose and we made our escape up the highway.

One more mustanging caper gone sour!

SPRUCE MOUNTAIN BILL

In 1965, I hired an old mustanger from Nevada called "Spruce Mountain Bill". He had sort of squatted in some of the buildings still standing from the early gold mining days.

He had five or six horses of his own plus his only means of support appeared to be trapping and selling a few mustangs. He had several ways of catching them but his most successful method was actually trapping them with coyote traps.

He would set traps in the mustang trails and "stud piles" and toggle them with light pole drags that he could follow and that would hopefully not break any legs.

He would follow the drag marks and then rope the wild horse and bring him back to his corral. He had an old one ton truck and when he got three or four he would haul them to Elko and sell them.

For those who don't know the meaning of "stud pile," it is where mustang stallions mark their territory to hopefully discourage other mustang bands from infringing on their range. They make huge piles of horse droppings every mile or so and every few days when they come by they add to the pile.

It would be similar to the way tom mountain lions mark their areas by making what is called a "scratch". The lions paw a small amount of pine or juniper needles and dirt under a tree along the borders of their claimed territory with the purpose of discouraging other lions from moving in on them. They urinate on the pile and the smell evidently lingers for up to several months.

I'm not sure how successful either method is but just giving you an idea of what happens.

Now Bill was always needing hay for his horses and I had a hay ranch about thirty miles away. Through the years Bill got further and further behind on what he owed me for hay. I decided the only way I would ever get anywhere near even was to see if I could get some labor in return for my outlay of the hay.

I needed to have some poles cut to build a hunting cabin at the Hotzel Ranch in Chamberlain Basin, Idaho. I had the ranch leased from the Idaho Department of Fish and Game as a base for my Chamberlain Basin Outfitters business. I needed a house for Joy and I and a place to cook for and house our guests.

My plan was to build a cabin about thirty by forty feet with a loft for sleeping quarters. The poles had to be cut green, skidded with horses about one quarter to one half mile across the meadow and creek. The lodgepole trees to cut were six or seven inches thru so a forty foot pole was pretty heavy. When they were at the site for the cabin they had to be hand peeled with a drawknife and laid straight and level to cure.

I propositioned Bill for the work trade, told him I would haul him and his horses plus some of mine to the Boy Scout camp at Cape Horn, northwest of Stanley and he could trail them on from there to Chamberlain where there was plenty of grass and feed for them.

The old Hotzel cabin is on the left. The new cabin featured in the Spruce Mountain Bill story is on the right. Both burned down in the forest fires of 2000.

I estimated probably ninety days to do the project. We would age and cure the poles for a year and build the cabin the second summer.

While Bill would be working on the poles, my father, Verl, myself, and other helpers would pour a concrete floor for the building. There are no tractors or concrete mixers allowed in there so we mixed and poured the concrete footings and floor for the cabin with shovels in a wheelbarrow! That makes for a long summer I can tell you for sure!

It took Bill ten days to get through, with lots of logged in and washed out trails. My famous old mule, Bernadine, abandoned him about half way through and went back about fifty miles and showed up at Stanley a few days later.

I had traded for her a few years before because they said she was unmanageable and they were going to kill her. She was an old mule then, with a US brand, and was said to have come to Nevada in 1941. We named her after a model in Los Angeles and she was an excellent pack mule up into the late 1970s – probably well over 40 years old when she retired, one of the best mules I have ever owned. She wintered out one winter on Big Creek and when my helper found her the next spring she was with a herd of mountain sheep and didn't want to leave them!

Bills' route would be roughly from Cape Horn, over thru Seafoam, down Rapid River to the Middle Fork of fhe Salmon River, down the Middle Fork to Marble Creek, up Marble Creek, down Monumental Creek, down Big Creek to the Dewey Moore ranch, up Coxie Creek, down to Moose Meadows and through Lodgepole Creek to Chamberlain Basin.

Bill had known Dewey Moore in their early years in Oregon I think. He stayed with Dewey a couple days to rest and regroup.

They radioed out about the lost Bernadine and that Bill was out of groceries. I made arrangements with Bob Fogg with Johnson Flying Service in McCall to deliver some groceries on the mail flight.

Dewey made the absolutely strongest coffee ever brewed. Joy and I found that out one stopover with him.

Bill got the pole job done by early September. Dad and Bill hadn't been hitting it off very well (understatement) and I knew I had to get Bill out of there to prevent major trouble.

Joy and I, along with guides Dick Hall and Fay Detweiler, would be in the Stoddard Creek country on a sheep hunt so I told Bill by radio phone to bring his stock across through the Root Ranch, Cold Meadows, Coyote Springs, Stoddard Creek, etc., and I would meet him at the pack bridge and make arrangements to get him and his stock back to Nevada.

We rendezvoused there and I told Bill I would get my horses back to Nevada and return for him and his stock.

He would just keep coming south by horseback up the Salmon River, up Panther Creek, down Morgan Creek and up the Salmon River again towards Stanley and Galena Summit. Somewhere along this route, I would meet him in a few days with an empty stock truck.

This is where the story gets very interesting!

I met Bill three or four days later just south of Stanley, Idaho. In his horse herd was one extra horse – a two-year-old, very nice Sorrel, well blooded Stallion.

Here is what Bill told me about how he got the horse. I have no idea if it is true but only what he related to me.

As he trailed his little horse herd along the route he come by a herd of loose horses. The little stallion sort of adopted Bills' horse covey and could not be discouraged to go back to his bunch. I'm not sure how hard Bill tried as he did like good horses.

Anyway, he caught the horse, which was broke to lead, and added it to his string. Sometime later an empty stock truck come by headed the same direction. The driver stopped to visit, asked Bill where he was headed and said, "I'm headed that way. I'll haul your horses as far as I am going."

Bill accepted, getting a free ride for twenty or thirty miles.

When I met up with Bill, saw the extra horse, heard the story and the description of the truck and driver it came together for me.

The guy had helped Bill steal his own horse!

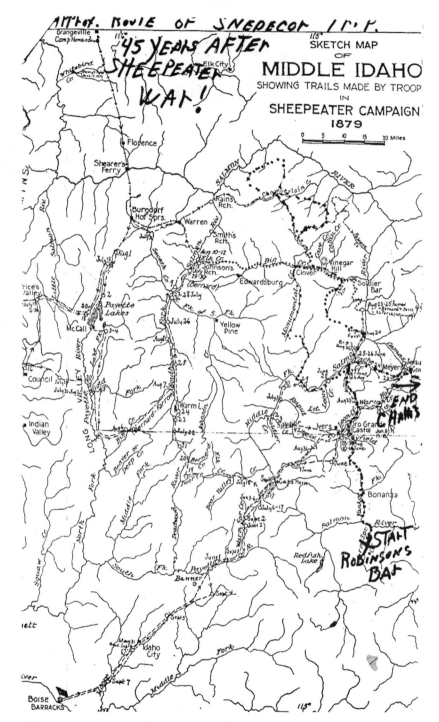

The approximate route of the Snedecor trip.

Chapter 19

1924 Outfitted Trip in The Frank Church Wilderness

P.C. "Pete" Snedecor, Author,
With Fred R. Johnson

Author's Note: This is the diary of Pete Snedecor and I'd like to provide some background on this unique diary of an early-day outfitted trip in what is now known as the "Frank Church River of No Return Wilderness."

The copy of this diary spans the time period from September 10, 1924, through December 4, 1914, and features a big game hunting trip on the area that is now the Frank Church Wilderness. The uniqueness of this story is that it was an outfitted trip by one of the earliest outfitters in Idaho, Tom Williams. Tom's trip into the back country started from Robinson Bar Ranch that was owned at that time by Chase Clark, Bethine Clark's father!

Morgan Williams of Challis, a descendant of Tom Williams, knew Pete Snedecor and said that although he didn't know how Mr. Snedecor came to be in Idaho, he lived out his life at the Thomas and Pistol Creek ranches. Pete must have returned to the country after the trip featured in the diary.

The back country trip covered over 317 miles and they met and purchased supplies from many of the early pioneers, including Dave Lewis on Big Creek, the Jeffries at the Stonebreaker Ranch in Chamberlain Basin and Warren Smith at Cold Meadows.

Good reading!!!

THE DIARY OF PETE SNEDECOR

September 10: Business of farewells at Johnson, Swopes and Fergusons. Off for the big trip at 8:45 a.m. Had good luncheon at Pismo, clam chowder and fried clams. Camped 2 miles north of Bradley on the Salinas River. Lots of wind and sand. Lamb chops for dinner and breakfast. Few stray doves; but no shooting.

September 11: Slow going through lots of traffic to a point 10 miles above Vallejo. Make camp in a prune orchard. One million and one mosquitoes and we don't know where they came from nor where they went. Probably starved to death after we left! Maneaters for fair and they "et" all night. Big T-bones for dinner and enjoyed them in spite of mosquitoes. Fred can eat more meat quicker than any whit many extant. Power to him. My appetite picking up, too, by the way!

September 12: Into Redding at noon. Shave and cards mailed to families. Took the Alturas road up the Pitt River and camped on a beautiful creek in the big timber, above Montgomery Creek. Found Modoc and Lassen Counties closed to hunting account of fire hazard; so our dreams of a buck in California went glimmering.

September 13: Sad and depressed business of driving all day through wonderful deer country and not being able to take a gun out of the car. Camped on a creek in a rancher's pasture just above Adin. Got a couple of bunnies just before sundown which made supper and breakfast.

September 14: Got a couple of ducks along the road and pulled them for dinner. Hit Alturas about noon and came up to Goose Lake country. Saw lots of geese along East side of lake. Crossed Oregon line and got hunting licenses. Drove around lake and camped at Youngs' Mill, where we had heard of good deer country. Tried it next A.M., but no luck, not even any sign.

September 15: Drove down to Harts' Ranch below Youngs' Mill and got talking with the old man. He invited us to camp in the yard and shoot geese from the ranch. Hunted a creek on the ranch and got several duck and quail and bunnies. Had the above for dinner. The old man regaled us with tales of pioneer days and of his former prowess with a rifle.

September 16: Walked over a hill towards a grain field to see about the geese. Only one bunch of Honkers came over and I got a double. These were dandy Canadas, weighing $11\frac{1}{2}$. Had lunch with Harts and invited for dinner. Accepted naturally! I got one more goose in the P.M. Also hunted the creek again and got duck and quail. Big goose dinner!

September 17: Up early and drove to same grain fields, about 3 miles from Hart's before daylight. I got 5 and Fred 3. He is feeling better over the goose proposition! Bid the Hart's goodbye, leaving them all the game except 2 geese. Drove to Lakeview for shave and bath, thank god!!! On up to Summer Lake and camped on the Bratten place. Will try for a buck under Winter Rien in the morning. Cut out the breast of the geese and fried 'em in butter. Oh Boy!!!

September 18: Tried for buck this A.M. but no luck. Also made a futile attempt for one this afternoon above camp. When we got back about sundown a peach of a Norther blew up and no chance to cook, so we banqueted on crackers and jam in the car, then made a dash for the beds and tried to keep from freezing and blowing away. Made it O.K. as we were all there in the A.M.

September 19: Moved camp ½ mile south to M.T. Jones' place. Put up the tent in case the Northers are chronic. Jones is 70 years old, a great hunter and packer.

September 20: Up before daylight and drove down to Curriers and up towards the reservoir. Auto blanket stiff named Hoover with us. Saw doe and 2 fawns. Fred jumped a couple of bucks but no shots. Lots of sign and good hunting ground. Plan to stay over and try it again in the morning. Hoover moves up to spring by reservoir and camps.

September 21: Up again early and down to reservoir. All set along rim when Mr. Hoover waltzes out and marches up and down the middle of reservoir, with our dog and jumps a buck which he doesn't see and is too far for us. This performance disgusts us with Oregon deer hunting and we plan to leave next day for Idaho.

September 22: Broke camp and drove north thru Siler Lake to Fort Rock and Ice Caves in Deschutes National Forest, where we camped. Fort Rock is old crater sticking up in the middle of the desert and very interesting and impressive looking. The Ice Caves are a lava blowout in the middle of a yellow pine forest.

September 23: Drove north to Bend. Burns Highway at Millican then east to Burns. Terrible road, nothing but lava, dust and sage. Rodeo on at Burns; but finally got a bed at Cole Hotel. Also made a barber shop and got shaves and baths which were badly needed. Could have gone down to OO Ranch for duck shooting; but decided time too short and plan to move on.

September 24: Glad to shake the dust of Burns from our feet and move east. Found "Oregon Highway 7" a parody of highways and endured 160 miles more of lava, dust and sage. Most of the lava rock and dust seemed to be in the middle of the road, and at times we had to stop to let the latter drift away before we could advance to the next emplacement of chuck holes! Finally reached Vale in the Malhuer River Valley, which seemed like paradise. Drove on to Boise down the east side of the Snake River Valley which is more paradise. Boise is pretty town of 20,000. Another big bath didn't hurt us any.

September 25: Drove to Twin Falls via Gooding where we presented Snopes letter to Purcht. He is Ford agent and very agreeable. Promised us good pheasant and duck shooting on our way back. Called on "Pop" Fisher but found him out of town. Due back at noon 26th so decided to stay over to see him. Met McGuire, his manager. Also met Ware who took us out while he worked some dogs. Earnest Whyte, a contractor, we found very pleasant. He has two Griffen dogs.

September 26: Met Fisher in the afternoon and found him to be a regular in every sense of the word. He fixed up our licenses. We are all set to meet Williams at Robinson's Bar tomorrow night. Robinson's Bar is on the Salmon, 16 miles below Stanley.

September 27: Early start for Stanley. Missed road once which took us 12 miles out of our way. Had lunch at Hailey, over Galena Summitt (8,752') to Stanley Basin. Arrived Stanley after dark and stayed at hotel. Telephoned the Bar we would arrive tomorrow.

September 28: Drove down to the Bar and found Williams had not arrived. The Bar great place owned by Chase Clark, attorney of Mackay. Hot Springs with plunge and fine log house with excellent accommodations. Marsh and his wife running place for him. First venison trip for dinner. Found we had broken our crankcase just above Stanley. Marsh is going to send it out for repairs while we are in the mountains.

September 29: Phone message saying Williams would arrive early. Went fishing up Warm Springs Creek and caught a few trout, stream pretty well fished out. I saw a fire over a mountain and when we got back to Bar found a ranger after horses to go to it. He elected me to accompany him. We climbed above the fire and decided we couldn't do any good, so started back down the mountain after dark. After the worst trip down thru rock slides and down-timber I ever experienced, we reached the bar at 10:30.

September 30: Williams arrived last night with the string and we got started at 10 a.m. There are four saddle animals and six pack animals. Frank McAuley is with Tom as wrangler and cook. Good horses and packs worked fine. We went back up to Sunbeam Dam and up the Yankee Fork to Sunbeam Mine. On over Loon Creek summit and camped at Frying Pan Flat on Loon Creek. Rained during the night but no damage done. Tom is great chap and it looks like a big trip. 23 miles.

October 1: Packed on down Loon Creek to Lost Packer Mine where

This picture was taken at Pinyon Peak Lookout, September 25, 1958. Pictured are Hazel Niece, Rose Hamilton, Pete Snedecor, Ella Boyle and Aileen Eberts.

auto road ends (12 miles). Then on down Loon Creek Trail to Warm Springs Creek where we camped. Rained again but nobody hurt. 20 miles. Total 43.

October 2: Packed 16 miles down Loon Creek to its mouth on the Middle Fork of Salmon. Camped 2 miles below junction on flat at Big Bend. Wind blowing and rainstorm during night, still nobody hurt. 18 miles. Total 61.

October 3: Fred and I tried out the fishing tackle in the river pools. Had a mess in no time. The Redsides or native Rainbow took flies fine. Tom and I climbed to top of ridge north of camp in the afternoon and spotted 3 goat about 1½ miles away. Plan to try for them tomorrow.

October 4: Tom, Fred and I hiked to top of ridge and ran into all the deer in the world! I killed a spike for meat. From now on we see deer every day in numbers from 10 to hundreds. Fred worked on up the ridge while Tom and I kept our level over into the canyon, after the goat which we had spotted again from the top. We jumped them in small timbers and bluffs and they gave us the slip and got back of us. Fred saw the proceeding from above and while Tom and I were battling down the canyon to the river and around to camp; Fred came down a ridge and met Mr. and Mrs. Goat. He got Billie at 650 yards and took Nannie in the right front foot. He got into camp after dark and told of the battle. We plan to go after Nannie and one of the kids for meat tomorrow.

October 5: We saddle 4 horses and all of us ride to top of ridge. Mac stays with animals and we go down to Billie. Spot Nannie and kids down in some bluffs. I play dog and circle below them and kick "em" off a ledge and drive "em" back up to Fred. Nannie is on 3 feet, Fred knocks her off a ledge and we get some good pictures. I take the largest kid for meat. Back to camp after dark. Tough trip.

October 6: Day of rest, baths, shaves and some fishing. I tried Tom's steel rod and spinner and got a 3½ lb. Dolly Varden. Fred got a bunch of Redsides on the fly.

October 7: Break camp and move down Middle Fork to Bernard Creek and turn North up Bernard after fording river at Curry's ranch. Beautiful canyon all the way down Middle Fork. Came 1½ miles up Bernard and camped.. Saw deer all along the way. 16 miles. Total 77.

October 8: Took a round for bucks. Fred goat a 375 lb. four point on the ridge east of camp. It had a sore on its back so no good for meat. Tom and I saw some big ones on Summit east of Bernard Creek; but didn't go up after them. Could see deer from camp anytime of day. "Mac" made mulligan out of rest of kid which was great.

October 9: Got started at 9:20 for the trip over Bernard Summit, down Soldier Creek and up 9000 feet to Soldier Summit. I took another spike for meat on Soldier Creek. Snow up to 16 inches deep on Soldier Creek Summit and beautiful view; Bitter Roots to east and Chamberlain Basin country to the north. Tough trail all day – rock, brush and grades. Camped (Pioneer Creek re: Stan Potts) 2 miles from Big Creek on account of darkness. 16 miles. Total 93.

October 10: Tom goes down to Lewis Ranch and got spuds and 10 lbs. of butter from pack outfit, who are leaving in couple of days. We packed up and moved down 2 miles past Lewis' on Big Creek and made a nice camp for 3 or 4 day stay. Tent up for first time. Weather still threatening and a drizzle now and then. C.P. Fordyce of "Outdoor Life" and Mr. Speed of Chicago, who compose the above mentioned party call in the afternoon. They were very much taken with the camp and outfit and got several pictures.

October 11: "Mac" and Fred stay in camp to fix up and clean up. Tom and I go goat prospecting down the creek a couple of miles and up canyon to north. Spotted 3 or 4 goats in bluffs on south side of Big

Creek. We circle over ridge back to camp. Saw 15 deer and I had standing shots from 30 to150 yards on all of them. Fred found the fish wouldn't rise to a fly.

October 12: Tom, Fred and I saddle up and go goat hunting. Rode up to top of a ridge to south of creek and Fred spotted a goat sleeping in canyon under us. Tom and he go after him and I circle around after one I had spotted on the other side of canyon. Fred started the battle at 1:45 and blasted Nannie 9 times. His front sight had been broken off so he was a little wild. Had her down then, so Tom went after her and finished the job. The firing ran my goat out of the canyon, so I worked up a good appetite.

October 13: Tom and I go up ridge just south of Soldier Bar after my goat. Climbed to top of mountain to snow where we got separated. We had seen one goat on ridge to west going up, so hiked down said ridge and kicked Nannie out of bed and poured a couple of loads into her. I had a fine time skinning her out and getting down the mountain. Found Tom waiting with tale of the big Billie he had seen coming down the ridge we went up. Tough luck we got separated.

October 14: Spent day in camp drying hides and cleaning up.

October 15: Packed and moved up Big Creek 3 miles to the mouth of Rush Creek and camped. Got a mess of trout out of Big Creek here. Tom and I went back to Lewis' after spuds and found the old man had killed a bear for Fordyce in the afternoon. He and Speed are leaving tomorrow via Yellow Pine. 3 miles. Total 100.

October 16: Early start and packed 14 miles up Big Creek and camped 1½ miles below mouth of Crooked Creek. Had to ford Big Creek seven times during the day.

October 17: Packed the 1½ miles to Crooked Creek and turned north up it 3 miles to the Jensen brothers cabin. Got 25 lbs. spuds here. Jensen had killed a bear in his back yard a couple of days before by setting a gun on bait. Came on up West Fork of Crooked Creek 7 miles and camped. While prospecting for elk, I saw a dandy 4 point buck near the trail and took it. Fred found fresh elk sign. We are now on the south edge of the elk country. 14 miles. Total 114.

October 18: "Mac" and I stayed in camp to pack the buck in and fix things up. Fred and Tom took a 12 mile round for elk. Found lots of sign and good country, no shots.

October 19: Tom, Fred and I ride up the head of West Fork and make a round for elk in the meadows. Lots of sign, but no elk. Decide to move camp up here tomorrow. Back late in camp where "Mac" had a big loin roast of buck ready. Some feeding!

October 20: Fred and I rode back up West Fork. Tom and "Mac" to bring camp up. I made some good elk country just west of Silver Creek. Lots of sign but "nary an elk." Got within 30 feet of big 4 point buck. Fred ranged around head of West Fork, but no luck. 6 miles. Total 132.

October 21: Hunted south of camp to top of ridge above Jensen's cabin. Fred and Tom jumped a calf elk. No luck.

October 22: Hunted meadow northwest of camp and swing around to east on ridge. Back in camp about 9:30 a.m. and decide to move on over to Moose Meadow. Packed 12 miles north to the meadows, formerly called Cold Meadows, because it freezes every day of the year. Found an old timer named Warren Smith camped on the east side of meadows. We moved on over to west side. Smith visited us tonight. He is in hunting elk for his winter's meat; but hasn't had any luck. 72 miles. Total 144.

October 23: Rode up ridge east of meadows. Tom and I hunted north side and jumped an elk in thick timber. No chance for a shot. Fred and Smith hunted up ridge. Country looks good, so decided to try it again tomorrow.

October 24: All four of us hunt the same country without success. Tom jumped a cow but didn't shoot.

October 25: Moved 14 miles north to West Fork of Chamberlain Creek. This is on north drainage of Chamberlain Basin, 4 miles north of Chamberlain Ranger Station. Tom and Smith go prospecting and report lots of elk sign. 14 miles. Total 158.

October 26: Smith and Fred hunted west of camp. Tom and I circled west and north. No luck.

October 27: Tom and I hunted west of West Fork. Fred and Smith to east. Fred and Smith came in at 4:30 p.m. having killed a cow elk each. Fred got his running at 110 yards after Smith had killed his standing at 40 yards. It started snowing last night and until we get out of the mountains it snows, rains and sleets intermittently. Disappears soon in canyons but is sticking on the summits.

October 28: Tom, "Mac", Smith and Fred take pack outfit to fetch in their kills. I struck out east to Dog Creek and hunt up it. Then down and swing back south of camp. Finally jumped 4 elk and killed a yearling bull. Got in camp just before dark and found that Smith couldn't go back to the dead elk. Snowed and rained all day.

October 29: Tom and I went for my elk and Smith walked back to locate the meat. I lost mine and had to hunt 2 hours to locate it. Smith also located and blazed a trail. Rain and snow.

October 30: Fred, Tom "Mac" and Smith took pack outfit and brought in the meat at 3 p.m. Wonderful meat.

October 31: Packed and moved to Moose Meadow. Gave the Jeffries at the old Stonebreaker Ranch the shoulders of Fred's cow. Smith took shoulders of my bull. Rain and snow. 14 miles. Total 172.

November 1: Packed 17 miles to south of Crooked Creek on Big Creek. Beautiful trip over West Fork Summit, 8000 feet, cold and clear and 16 inches new snow. Smith is guiding and took wrong ridge down to Jensens' cabin. Tom had to take charge and we had tough time bucking down steep mountain with no trail and full pack. 17 miles. Total 189.

November 2: Bid Smith and Leo goodbye. He goes up Big Creek over Elk Summit tomorrow. We ford Big Creek and pack 16 miles up Monumental Creek towards Thunder Mountain. Camped 3 miles below Roosevelt. 16 miles. Total 205.

November 3: Got started at 10 a.m. to go over Thunder Mountain. Turned up Mule Creek at old mining camp of Roosevelt. It was established in 1902 during the Thunder Mountain gold rush. Half a mountain slid down Mule Creek Canyon in 1904 and dammed Monumental Creek and flooded the town of Roosevelt. It is now under 30 feet of water. We passed the Dewey Mine and lost an hour on the wrong trail. Finally got straightened out and crossed the mountain, passed the Sunnyside Mine and Bellco Mill down to Marble Creek. Camped 8 miles below summit on Marble. Found only 16 to 18 inches of snow on summit. 15 miles. Total 220.

November 4: Snow and rain greeted us again this morning. We moved 4 miles down Marble to Mink Creek and camped. Got the tent up and big fire going. Snowed all afternoon. 4 miles. Total 224.

November 5: Four inches snow on ground this morning and still at it. Half rain and half snow in the canyon, but we know the snow is piling up on the summits. No chance to hunt or move.

November 6: Got things dry enough to pack and moved 12 miles down Marble to get below snow and hunt buck. Camped at Buck Camp ½ mile above Bear Creek. Snowed and rained in flurries all day. 12 miles. Total 236.

November 7: "Mac" and I went 5 miles down Marble to Mitchells' Ranch for provisions. No one home so we borrowed 2 days rations of flour. Telephoned to Camerons' Ranch regarding Loon Creek Summit. Reported 6 to 8 feet of snow. Fred went up on ridge east of camp and jumped a big 4-5 point buck. Got him running at 150 yards. Took head for trophy, but meat was musky. We dissected the rest of the elk meat in the afternoon and started smoking it.

November 8: Snowed 4 inches wet snow last night. Tom and Fred went up ridge east of camp and looked for big heads. They saw 60 to 75 deer and could have killed 20 buck. Didn't see the head they wanted tho; so didn't make a kill. I went around south and east of same ridge to get camp meat. Killed what I thought to be a 2 point, but found it to be a doe with horns. Packed the horns in and told of the freak. Decide it's worth taking of. Snowed wet snow all afternoon.

November 9: Snow 6 inches deep this A.M. After rain and snow all night. Decide no chance to move today; so Tom and I go after the freak head. Back at 2 p.m. wet to the skin. Snowing and raining steadily all day. Sixteen inches wet snow on ridge just above camp. We have to move tomorrow rain or shine, no flour, sugar, coffee, or baking powder.

November 10: Still snowing but signs of breaking. Packed a wet camp and got started at 11:40. Down Marble six mile to Middle Fork. Then down Middle Fork 11 miles to Camerons' Ranch. Arrived after dark and got supper at ranch. No place to sleep in house or barn, so we bed down on 4 inches frozen snow. It has cleared off and the mercury is flirting with zero. Saw hundreds of deer all day on their winter range on north side of Middle Fork. 17 miles. Total 253.

November 11: Up at daylight. Everything frozen tight, but slept warm. Breakfast in ranch house. Bought supplies and got away at 9:30. Moved to old camp at Big Bend below mouth of Loon Creek. Loon Creek Summit closed account of 10 feet snow, so we have to go up Camos Creek over Morgan Creek Summit and out by Challis. Fred killed a 4 point buck on south side of river, but one point broken. The running season on in full tilt, deer everywhere. The Middle Fork country is their winter range and bucking range. The country is freezing up. Smaller creeks frozen over and Middle Fork has shore ice out 10 to 20 feet and running full of slush ice.

November 12: "Mac" and I stayed in camp and Tom and Fred go up ridge north of camp after a herd. They got back at 3 p.m. with wonderful head, 9 points on one side and 10 on other. They saw any number of bucks and one actually charged Tom. Tom made no false moves tho, so Mr. Buck stopped within 30 feet of him. That doe with the horns proved to be the toughest meat imaginable, so we are using some of the smoked elk meat today.

November 13: Broke camp and packed down to mouth of Camos Creek and 6 miles up it. Meet old timer named Frank Allison guiding two dudes from Idaho Falls and camped near them. No horse feed here and decide not to hunt for sheep, too risky, warned by Jones on Middle Fork. Decide to go up to Allison's Ranch tomorrow and out behind him over the summit the next day. 17 miles. Total 280.

November 14: Moved up to Allison's Ranch on Silver Creek. We ate in house with him and bunked in house. Got horse feed which they needed badly. Allison has nice little dude ranch. Radio, bath, etc. Snowing today. 12 miles. Total 292.

November 15: Got early start and went 25 miles over Morgan Creek summit down to Oyler's Ranch. Found 2 ½ feet snow on top. Weather cleared as soon as got over top and it felt good to get out of storms. Had fine dinner at Oyler's. Fred and I bedded down in saddle room. Cold and clear. Mercury bumping 0 every night. 25 miles. Total 317.

November 16: Stock badly stove up, but we make it to Challis. Found fair accommodations at Garland Hotel. Kelly, the game warden, greeted us and looked over the trophies.

November 17: Horses so crippled, can't move today. Trip officially ends here. Tom paid off and he plans to bring string to Gus Sargeants 14 miles up Salmon River tomorrow. "Mac" and I hike 4 miles over to hot springs for much needed bath.

November 18: Fred and I get stage at 7:30 and go up to Robinson's Bar for car. Cold ride. Salmon full of ice. McDougal, the parson from Arco, came in at dark. He and Marsh are only men who ever ran the Salmon River in a canoe. They went from the Bar to Riggins in 1923.

November 19: Late breakfast. Found car fixed and got started at 22:30. Snowing again and roads frozen and slippery. Arrived at Gus' at 3 P.M. and packed car for trip out.

November 20: Drove to Arco today. We are taking "Mac" and Nein with us to Twin Falls.

November 21: On into Twin over a thawed road that was sticky as chewing gum. Arrived Twin safely and happy over a wonderful trip and over the prospects of pheasant shooting. Returned to Los Angeles December 4th via Ely,. Tonopah, Goldfield and Owens Valley.